# Gunshots forced Jack to duck back into the burning cabin.

He slammed the door shut and moved away as fast as he could. Hayley and the others, who were behind him when he opened the door, quickly retreated back to where they'd been.

*Now what?*

The heat from the fire was nearly unbearable.

"We have to at least *try* to get out through the bedroom window—we've got no other choice," Hayley said. "This time, I'll go first."

Jack couldn't let her do it. The first one out would be the most vulnerable to getting shot.

"You're working on *my* team," Jack said. "*I* make the decisions."

"You can believe that if you want to," Hayley said.

Jack was more stunned than angry. People just didn't talk to him like that.

He followed her to the bedroom where she grabbed a small bedside table and swung it to break the glass.

As he feared, her efforts were greeted with gunfire. They both hit the ground...

**Jenna Night** comes from a family of Southern-born natural storytellers. Her parents were avid readers and the house was always filled with books. No wonder she grew up wanting to tell her own stories. She's lived on both coasts but currently resides in the Inland Northwest, where she's astonished by the occasional glimpse of a moose, a herd of elk or a soaring eagle.

## Books by Jenna Night

### Love Inspired Suspense

#### Range River Bounty Hunters

*Abduction in the Dark*
*Fugitive Ambush*

#### Rock Solid Bounty Hunters

*Fugitive Chase*
*Hostage Pursuit*
*Cold Case Manhunt*

*Last Stand Ranch*
*High Desert Hideaway*
*Killer Country Reunion*
*Justice at Morgan Mesa*
*Lost Rodeo Memories*
*Colorado Manhunt*
"Twin Pursuit"

Visit the Author Profile page at LoveInspired.com.

# FUGITIVE AMBUSH

## JENNA NIGHT

**LOVE INSPIRED** SUSPENSE
INSPIRATIONAL ROMANCE

**LOVE INSPIRED** SUSPENSE
INSPIRATIONAL ROMANCE

ISBN-13: 978-1-335-58794-7

Fugitive Ambush

Copyright © 2022 by Virginia Niten

For questions and comments about the quality of this book, please contact us at CustomerService@Harlequin.com.

Love Inspired
22 Adelaide St. West, 41st Floor
Toronto, Ontario M5H 4E3, Canada
www.LoveInspired.com

Printed in U.S.A.

Have not I commanded thee? Be strong and of a good courage; be not afraid, neither be thou dismayed: for the Lord thy God is with thee withersoever thou goest.
—*Joshua* 1:9

For my mom, Esther. Always.

# ONE

The tiny hairs on the nape of bounty hunter Hayley Ryan's neck stood on end and a ripple of goose bumps moved across the surface of her skin.

Someone was behind her.

Probably the stone-cold killer she was pursuing.

Taking aim at her right now.

She was in the forest on the west side of the town of Blue Mountain, Idaho, helping track down two-time murderer and bail jumper Barry Foster.

A month ago a relative purchased a bond to get Foster out of jail after he'd been arrested on theft charges. Following his release, the cops got the evidence they needed to charge him with murder and his bail bond was revoked. But before anyone could find him he executed a second man, possibly a witness to the initial killing.

And then he'd vanished.

Cops and bounty hunters all over the region were looking for the guy.

Jack Colter, owner of Eagle Rapids Bail Bonds, located in nearby Range River, had jumped into the chase for Foster with a vengeance. He had ongoing cases and his bounty hunter staff was spread thin. He'd asked Hayley for assistance, which surprised her. The two agencies were fiercely competitive. She didn't especially care for Jack, who was known as a rule-breaker in the professional bounty hunting community. But this particular bad guy *really* needed to be caught, so she'd agreed to join forces with him.

Haley heard several more twigs breaking and footfalls behind her.

Her gaze flickered across the shadowy forest surrounding her as instinct, packing a punch as teeth-rattling as any physical blow, screamed at her to do something. *Now.*

The Eagle Rapids bounty hunter she'd been paired with while working this case, Luther Garcia, was thirty feet ahead of her and slightly to her right. Dappled sunlight, filtering through the leaves and pine boughs laced together overhead, highlighted his long brown hair shot through with gray. On the cusp of retirement, Luther wanted one more big capture before calling it quits on fieldwork and transitioning to a desk job.

They'd gotten a tip about campers in the area, and she and Luther had decided to check it out. Because Foster himself had not specifically been sighted, she'd held off on asking Jack and the other two bounty hunters in Blue Mountain to drop what they were doing and meet up with them.

That had been a mistake.

Hayley knew that now, all the way down to the pit of her knotted stomach. Because the twig-snapping sounds and footfalls behind her were speeding up and getting closer. Spinning around while firing several shots might be a cool move on a TV show, but real life was so much more complicated than that.

Were the sounds coming from an innocent bystander enjoying a hike? Or were they coming from the human predator she was trying to capture? Foster might be aiming his weapon at her, ready to start shooting the second she slowed down, turned to look behind her or gave any indication that she was aware she was being stalked.

Hayley's hands shook. She did her best to steady them.

Luther needed to know something was wrong. His attention was focused on a foliage-filled ravine as he searched for tracks potentially left by their fugitive.

Tension tightened like barbed wire around Hayley's midsection. Sweat beaded across her forehead despite the coolness of the temperature.

She needed to get her hand closer to her gun without attracting attention. She also needed to get Luther's attention.

*Lord, help!* Not exactly an eloquent prayer, but a heartfelt one.

She had to take action. The sounds behind her were getting closer. There wasn't time to be subtle.

She took a breath and shouted, "Luther, get down!"

The sound of her own voice still rang in her ears as she drew her gun and spun around. Holding her fire, she dropped to make herself a smaller target.

She spotted a figure barely twenty feet away, in a small clearing where the sunlight filtered into the forest. It was her bail jumper, Barry Foster. Red stubble grew across his head and his upper lip and chin. Dressed in khakis and a plaid long-sleeved shirt, he didn't look like a desperate fugitive on the run, which made him all the more dangerous to the general public. He looked like any other citizen you might see out and about in any neighborhood except for the narrowed, malevolent expression in his eyes and the cold, joyless smirk on his lips.

And the gun he held pointed Hayley.

He fired.

Hayley crouched and darted sideways, toward the ravine and Luther, while Foster continued firing. She reached the ravine and dove in, landing hard on her shoulder. Taking advantage of the brush and tall wild grasses, she flattened her body and gave herself a couple of seconds to catch her breath.

Then she rose up just enough so she could return fire and prevent Foster from getting any closer. She took aim at him as he turned his head from side to side, looking for her. But before she could squeeze the trigger she saw a flicker of movement through the foliage behind him. And then more movement beside him.

There were other people in the woods following her besides Foster. They were all moving, and now Hayley couldn't get a clear shot at any of them.

Hayley backed into the ravine. She glanced over and saw gray hair amid the greenery. Luther. He was lying on the side of the ravine, head barely above the edge, gun drawn and pointed in the direction of Foster and the others.

"You okay?" Luther whispered as she crawled toward him.

Hayley nodded. "Don't know if you noticed, but there are people other than Foster out there."

"Time to call in the troops and get some help," Luther said in his signature low gravelly voice. He reached for his phone.

*Bang! Bang!*

Bullets shot through the brambles and grass and then hit the dirt inches from the spot where Hayley and Luther were hiding. Rapid footfalls and snapping twigs made it clear that Foster and the other two people were headed in their direction.

*Bang!*

"Go!" Luther gestured toward the end of the ravine away from the shooters. "You're younger and faster. Find us a spot where we can hunker down long enough to call for help."

"I'm not going to leave you here."

"Well, I'm not planning on staying here," Luther growled. "I didn't make it through this many years as a bounty hunter because I give up easily. I'll just be a little ways in back of you. I want you to focus on finding the best direction to go while I make sure nobody sneaks up on us from behind. Now, *move!*"

Keeping low, Hayley ran forward, paying scant attention to the sharp branches and thorns that scratched her skin and caught her hair as she moved. As promised, Luther followed at a distance, pausing at intervals to glance behind them.

Hayley looked around as she ran, desperate to find a good option. And then she saw it. A cluster of trees growing alongside a large granite outcropping the size of a two-story house. If they could just get over to the trees and behind the outcropping without being seen, they could hide and make their call for help.

*Bang! Bang!*

Hayley heard the heavy steps of Luther coming up behind her. Keeping her attention focused on her path, she quickly told him her plan before starting a sprint toward the cluster of trees and the stone outcropping.

She made it! Squeezing between the pine

trees and the giant chunk of granite, she moved around the rock until she was behind it and out of view of the shooters.

From the corner of her eye she saw Luther moving toward her around the curve of the rock. A cautious wave of relief passed over her.

The grizzled bounty hunter dropped down into a sitting position beside her.

"I'll keep my gun at the ready while you call for help," Hayley said, her gaze fixed toward the edge of the rock while she watched for bad guys.

Luther made a sound, but she didn't understand it. She turned to him and saw blood. Lots of it. It looked like he'd been shot.

"Luther," she said softly. "Hang on. I'll get us some help." She grabbed her phone and tapped it several times to connect with Jack. He and the rest of the crew would be able to respond faster than anybody else. And while they were on their way they could alert law enforcement and emergency medical services.

"Come on, *come on*!" Hayley whispered fiercely as her phone offered up a staticky sound and not much else. She turned her attention back to Luther where a quick check revealed a shot to his right side and leg. She did her best to stop the bleeding with a wadded-up scarf.

Luther slumped forward.

Again, she tried to make a call but it didn't go through.

She heard Foster's voice. He and his cohorts were getting closer. They must be following the trail that she and Luther had inevitably left behind them.

Fear twisted her gut as she looked at Luther. Pushing him to start moving again when he was injured and losing blood was not an optimal idea. But staying put would get the both of them killed.

"I'm on my way. Stay where you are and keep the line open. Do not disconnect." Jack Colter kept his voice calm as he hit the gas pedal of his truck and made a beeline down Falcon Drive toward the opposite end of Blue Mountain where he knew Hayley and Luther had been looking around in the woods beside the park. If he picked up a police escort on the way because he was speeding, so much the better. Twice his phone had chimed with his screen indicating that Hayley was on the line, but when he answered he'd only gotten dead air. On the third try, the call had finally gone through.

"We followed the big ravine north." Hayley's voice was beginning to break up. Cell reception could be tricky in remote Idaho towns like Blue Mountain. "There's a granite outcropping to the west. Luther and I made it that far." There was an interruption of static, and then he heard her say the words, "Right away."

"I'm almost there," he assured her.

"I said we need *medical assistance* right away," she said, sounding frustrated. "Luther was shot. Looks like multiple times."

Jack's stomach dropped. He'd known Luther for a good chunk of his life. Twenty years, at least. The man was like a member of his family. Luther and his wife, Jessica, were looking forward to welcoming their first grandchild in just three months.

"Do what you can to stop any bleeding and keep him still," Jack ordered. "Help is on the way."

"We have to move," Hayley said, sounding frantic. "I think Foster and the two men who are with him have figured out where we are. They're heading our way. They're almost on us."

The call disconnected.

Jack's truck slid to a stop in the loose gravel after he hit the brakes near the spot where Hayley had parked her SUV. He punched 9-1-1 into his phone to quickly report what was happening and ask for help. He ignored the operator's request for him to stay on the line. With law enforcement and emergency medical on the way, he needed to talk to the other two bounty hunters he had working here in Blue Mountain.

He tapped his phone's screen and while it rang he grabbed an electronic tablet from the passenger seat. At the moment he was getting decent reception, but there was no telling what it would be like once he started hiking into the forest. He opened the topographic map on the tablet and quickly found the rock outcropping Hayley had referred to.

"Yeah?" Bounty hunter Milo Keach answered on the other end of the call after a couple of rings.

Jack tossed the tablet back onto the passenger seat, slid out of the truck and grabbed his utility belt with his weapons and handcuffs and snapped it on. All the while he gave Milo a recap of what was going on.

"Katherine and I will be right there," he said when Jack was done.

Jack disconnected and grabbed a handheld radio that picked up local emergency band frequencies.

He strapped on a bulletproof vest as he started to move across the tree line into the forest. Pine branches thick with needles slapped at his face as he picked up the clear trail left by several individuals walking together. He stepped forward, as stealthily as possible, and it wasn't long before he spotted the ravine. He stayed several yards to the west of it, heading north, toward where the map had indicated the stone outcropping would be.

He stopped several times to listen and maybe hear where the bad guys were. Hopefully, they were not with Hayley and Luther, but he had to be ready for that possibility. While this was rugged mountain terrain, it was under a mile away from the edge of the sprawling lakeside town. So he could faintly hear car engines and the occasional dog barking or human voice.

Continuing to make his way forward, he forced himself to scan his surroundings rather than getting tunnel vision and focusing only on finding the outcropping. The last thing he wanted to do was walk into an ambush. Eventually he spotted his target, a speckled grayish monolith of stone. His heart sank. The wild grasses around it were stomped down indicating that the bail jumper and his companions had likely found Hayley and Luther's hiding place.

He heard sirens at the same time that he saw the first drops of blood on the grass.

*Luther.*

*Please, Lord, save him*, Jack prayed silently while forcing himself to take a steadying breath.

He moved forward and saw more blood. Waiting for law enforcement to arrive didn't seem like the best option, not when both of the two bounty hunters were in grave danger and Luther's life could be slipping away. Jack continued walking.

He approached the edge of the outcropping with his gun drawn and he stepped around it to have a look, still holding on to the unreasonable hope that Hayley and Luther would be safely hidden back there. But he didn't see anyone. Just more trampled wild grass and blood.

A frightening amount of blood.

Disappointment dropped a cinder block in his chest. So much for hoping he would find Hayley and Luther quickly, and that Luther's injury would turn out not to be so bad.

And then the thought occurred to him: What if this patch of blood didn't only belong to Luther? What if Hayley had been shot, too?

He had to find them. Quickly.

He scanned the area, searching for a trail to follow. Foster must have taken the bounty hunters captive and forced them to walk somewhere. He could hear law enforcement vehicles arriving near the area where he had parked. He keyed the radio and let them know where he was and what he'd seen. An officer who knew the bounty hunters were in town confirmed that he'd heard Jack's transmission.

Jack turned his focus back to looking for a trail to follow, moving deeper into the wilderness while scanning the ground. He'd only gone ten yards when he heard gunfire and someone yelling. Unexpectedly, the sounds came from the direction of town.

He turned eastward, moving away from the wilderness and back in that direction. His path intersected a trail left in the grass showing more drops of blood. The bad guys must have taken the bounty hunters this way or they'd managed to get away and were headed toward a population center and help. Farther ahead, the forest would end where it met with a city park.

Jack was almost there when he realized the trail he'd been following now split into two, with the fainter one making a sharp left turn and looping back into the forest. Torn between following the sounds from the direction of town and following the trail back into the woods, he hesitated. Figuring that cops would respond to the gunfire in town, he made the decision to turn back into the forest. After taking a few steps he nearly stumbled over Luther's outstretched legs. The veteran bounty hunter was seated on the ground, leaning against Hayley. She had one arm wrapped protectively around him as she held her gun at the ready, looking terrified but determined.

"Don't shoot," Jack said, afraid of startling her as he dropped down beside her. The relief he felt at finding them alive was immediately undermined by stark fear when he saw how severely Luther had been injured. The man was barely conscious.

"We had to move," Hayley said, speaking quietly. "It was hard on Luther, but Foster and his two pals were heading directly toward us. They were fast and Foster was calling out that they were going to kill us. He said he knew the cops would never stop hunting for him. But if some bounty hunters were killed in the pursuit, that would put a stop to any civilian helping in his capture. They'd be too afraid."

Her voice was tight with tension, but it was otherwise steady. The hand holding her gun was also steady. She was a strong woman. Courageous. Jack appreciated that. She'd made a tough decision and taken action. He admired that, too.

Too bad she didn't think too highly of *him*. But he understood why.

"We left an obvious trail making it look like we were heading into town and then snuck back over here," she continued, speaking fast. "Anyway, we were able to trick them. When they got to the edge of the park and realized they'd lost us, one of them started yelling and firing shots back in this direction."

Jack heard sirens approaching, obviously cops responding to the gunshots at the nearby park. Furious at what the thugs had done to his bounty hunters, Jack wanted to go after Foster and his companions. But getting Luther immediate medical attention was the clear priority. He keyed his radio and requested emergency care for a patient with multiple gunshot wounds. He gave the dispatcher directions to drive across the grass on the city park until they reached the edge of the forest, about ten yards from Luther's location in the woods.

"You go flag them down while I stay here with Luther," Jack said to Hayley. She'd be safer with the cops when they arrived.

Jack wanted to stay with Luther, who was now unconscious, and pray for him. If this was the moment when his friend would be passing away, then Jack wanted to be by his side.

"We'd have to move him if I go," Hayley said quietly, dark blue eyes focused on him as she nodded to Luther's prone body propped against her. "That's not a good idea."

She was right.

"Okay, I'll go."

"If you see the fugitives, don't fire at them unless someone's life is in danger and you absolutely have to," Hayley said. "Don't try to get revenge for what happened to Luther."

A grim smile crossed Jack's lips. Hayley clearly believed the rumors that Jack was lacking in professional ethics. The entire Ryan clan probably shared her low opinion of him. He sighed. Even if he had the time to do it now, explaining the truth to people never seemed to work so he'd given up on it. Let them believe the worst.

"Be right back," he said, turning to fetch the emergency medical crew already making their way toward them.

He quickly found them and led them back to Luther, where they stabilized the wounded man and loaded him into their vehicle.

As soon as the ambulance departed, Jack called Milo and Katherine, who were with the law enforcement officers still in the forest. Katherine volunteered to phone Luther's wife to let her know what had happened.

Getting ready to follow the ambulance to the hospital, Jack looked around for Hayley. She was sitting at one of the park's picnic tables, phone in hand, exhaustion made evident by her slumped posture. He walked toward her.

*Bang! Bang! Bang!*

Splinters flew up from the picnic table where Hayley was sitting. Two more shots followed, these also obviously aimed at her. She dove to the ground and crawled behind a cluster of pine trees.

Jack and the cops took cover.

As soon as there was a pause in the gunfire, Jack raced toward Hayley and hit the dirt beside her. He risked a quick look around and caught a brief glimpse of Barry Foster before the bail jumper disappeared around a building. He didn't see the other two assailants.

In patrol cars and on foot, the cops sped in the direction where Foster had disappeared.

"You okay?" Jack said to Hayley, helping her up.

She nodded, and he was glad to see no evidence of injury.

It was bad enough that Luther had been gravely wounded. Now it looked like their fugitive had singled out Hayley Ryan as a target for murder.

# TWO

By ten o'clock that evening Jack felt like a week had passed by.

Now back at his office in downtown Range River, he sat on the edge of his desk and surveyed his Foster capture team who were now scattered around the room. Well, *some* of his team were there. Luther was in the ICU at the county hospital in Range River, transferred there after being stabilized at the medical facility in Blue Mountain. He'd lost a lot of blood and had to have a transfusion before the doctors could begin surgery to remove the bullets and repair the damage to his body.

Hayley Ryan sat in a chair in front of him. He considered her a member of his team even though she was not his actual employee.

Normally, Eagle Rapids Bail Bonds and the Range River crew competed against one another, rather intensely, which Jack enjoyed.

They didn't chase after fugitives who had been bonded out of jail by the other bail bond business.

Other than following that basic unspoken rule, any time a bail jumper was suspected to be in the area, both teams went after the fugitive full throttle. So of course they often stepped on each other's toes. Not a problem for Jack. He enjoyed the competition and was more interested in getting results than in playing nice with other bounty hunters. Being thought of as an easy-to-get-along-with kind of guy wasn't part of his public image, anyway.

Not that he'd intentionally crafted the impression people had of him. That he was a cold-blooded bounty hunter who habitually broke the law while doing his job yet somehow managed to get away with it. But the rumors and innuendos, based on lies originated and fueled by people he'd captured and put back into jail, had started early in his career.

All bounty hunters faced this to one degree or another, but in Jack's case, the problem had been compounded when he' kicked in a door at a fugitive's sister's house, believing the man was about to harm her. He'd saved the woman and caught the perp, but family loyalty meant she'd stuck by her brother's story when the man claimed Jack had acted unethically and had violently invaded her home for no good reason. That meant quite a few people had a bad impression of him. People like Hayley Ryan, for instance.

He'd tried to address them directly, tell the truth and explain the facts. Other than the people close to him, who actually knew him, nobody believed what he'd said. Eventually he reached the point where he realized it was probably smarter to let that shady reputation work for him. In some situations it did seem to intimidate bad guys and make it easier to subdue them, so he'd tried to make the best of it.

"How are you holding up?" he asked Hayley after he took a couple of bracing sips of strong black coffee.

For the last few minutes, Hayley had been sitting looking off into the distance, at nothing in particular as far as Jack could tell. She was rattled by the events of the day and he didn't blame her. *He* was rattled. But throughout the afternoon and evening, while the others had planned and talked, expressing their outrage over what had happened in Blue Mountain, their astonishment that Foster would linger at the scene to take shots at Hayley with cops nearby and their grave concerns for Luther, Hayley hadn't said much of anything.

Jack knew from experience, as a combat veteran and as a bounty hunter, that keeping your emotions bottled up after a traumatic event was not good.

Hayley turned her gaze toward him. Her dark blue eyes were filled with fury. "I know I messed up," she said in a low voice. "I know what happened to Luther was my fault."

Jack had been there. He knew how self-recrimination felt. Like a knife to the heart. A rusty one.

He was beyond grateful that none of the shots fired at Hayley had struck her. Even the ones fired by Foster while they were in the park had missed her. She had some scrapes and small cuts from the day's ordeals, but she was physically okay.

Nevertheless, the emotional injury was significant. And it couldn't be allowed to fester while she kept quiet.

"I've always thought you Ryans believed you were better than everybody else. Guess this proves it."

Her eyebrows shot up until they nearly disappeared beneath her reddish-blond bangs. "What did you just say to me?"

Her words were slow and deliberate. Like she was fighting to keep herself from knocking him out.

Good.

He took another sip of coffee. "Tell me, Hayley *Ryan*, do you really believe you could have controlled everything that happened today?" He shook his head. "Man, what an ego."

He watched the expression on her face turn from anger to confusion to disbelief.

"What are you talking about?" she asked, her voice taking on a squeaky, indignant tone.

"My point of view is that it's all on Barry Foster. And the men who were with them. They were the ones with the guns doing the shooting. But you seem to think you could have somehow controlled that. Or prevented it. Or used your superpowers or something." He shrugged.

She threw her hands up. "I'm not claiming I could have controlled everything. I just wish…that I'd reacted better. Or kept an eye out for anybody potentially following us in the forest. I wish I'd done *something* so that Luther didn't get shot." She shook her head. "I should have been smarter. More vigilant."

"You should have been perfect, maybe?" he

asked before setting his coffee mug down beside him. "Because all of you bounty hunters from Range River Bail Bonds are perfect?"

She sighed heavily. "I'm already tired of this. If you have a point, would you just state it?"

"If I had been in the same situation you were in, I can't think of anything I would have done differently. Beating yourself up isn't going to help Luther or anybody else. I specifically requested *your* assistance on this case because I believed in your skills as a bounty hunter and that hasn't changed. You and I haven't worked together before, but your success in capturing bail jumpers is a matter of public record."

All but two of Jack's bounty hunters had been wrapped up in other cases when the Barry Foster search began. While he was trying to figure out how he could get involved in the chase, word came out that Hayley Ryan had located Foster on the outskirts of Range River and had nearly captured him single-handedly before he got away.

Jack had contacted her and suggested they work together. She'd agreed, sharing intel she had that Foster might be hiding in the Blue Mountain area. So she'd joined up with his team and they'd headed in that direction this morning.

"Any bounty hunter could have gotten caught in the situation you and Luther found yourselves in," Jack added. But not just anybody could have kept their cool like she had and gotten herself and her partner out of the situation alive. He gave her a slight nod. "You did okay, kid."

*"Kid?"* The indignant tone was back in her voice.

Jack didn't bother holding back a grin, which appeared to annoy her even more.

She was a lot younger than him. Fifteen years younger. She still showed signs of youthful hope and optimism. Both traits he'd consciously squashed within himself a long time ago after realizing that they were of no practical use to him. Not after his wife left him and he realized that facing life with an attitude of cynicism and grim practicality made things go a lot more smoothly.

Plus it helped keep him alive when he was hunting bad guys.

Milo and Katherine Keach, the husband-and-wife bounty hunters who'd been in Blue Mountain along with Hayley and Jack, walked over toward the main area of the office from the kitchenette each carrying a mug of coffee and sat down on a sofa. Both were skilled at their jobs, but given Foster's propensity for violence Jack had wanted at least one more person on the capture crew when they went after him.

"I heard you talking a couple of minutes ago," Milo said to Hayley. "No one's blaming you for what happened to Luther."

"This is a dangerous, unpredictable job," Katherine added after a sip of coffee. "You take chances with no guarantee of the outcome. I know Luther hasn't regained consciousness yet, but I'm sure he doesn't hold you accountable for what happened. The blame falls squarely on the shoulders of the thugs who tried to kill you two."

Jack glanced down at the tips of his cowboy boots and nodded. Milo and Katherine truly cared about people. And despite the competition between his Eagle Rapids Bail Bonds and the Ryans' Range River Bail Bonds, his people knew when to offer grace and kindness to a colleague trying to do the same tough job.

When he looked up, Hayley's chin was lifted. Her shoulders were straighter and she offered a slight nod of gratitude to Milo and Katherine. That was a good sign.

"I know we're all tired, so I'll keep this meeting short," Jack said. "Right now, the doctors are doing all they can for Luther." Fear over the possibility that his old friend might not make it squeezed his heart. He took a steadying breath and cleared his throat. "If any of you would rather stay back, maybe hang around the hospital with Jessica over the coming days, I'm okay with that. I can call around and find other bounty hunters to help out with the pursuit." His goal was to give Hayley a way out if she wanted it.

"We're still in the chase," Katherine said, exchanging glances with her husband.

"I'm still in, too," Hayley said.

Jack turned his attention toward her. "Sleep on that and let me know for sure tomorrow."

She crossed her arms defensively over her chest. "Why? Do you not really believe that little speech you just gave that was supposed to boost my morale? At least I think that's what the point of it was. I'm not really sure." She gave him a pointed look. "Anyway, do you not want me along tomorrow because the truth is you *don't* think I'm capable of doing the job? Or are you afraid you'll end up partnered with me and I'll get you shot?"

"I'm going to say *no* on all of the above,"

Jack answered easily. Because it was the truth. He had not lost faith in her abilities. "But Barry Foster went out of his way to target you personally in the park. Maybe you bruised his ego because you came so close to capturing him. *Twice.* And that's why he wants you dead. Or it could be for some other reason. In any event, that's a lot of wrath directed at you from a criminal who's killed two people already. For the sake of your own safety, you might want to step away from this case."

"No." She shook her head, dismissing the idea. "I've had bail jumpers angry at me before."

"To this extent? Did they double back to a crime scene to shoot at you with cops *right there*?"

Hayley tightened her arms across her chest and leaned back in her chair. "After all that's happened, now that Luther is in the hospital fighting for his life, I'm twice as determined to capture Foster. If you don't want me working with you, fine. I'll figure out something else."

It was hard for Jack to argue with her because if he were in her situation he would feel the same way.

"If you want to continue working with us, I'm good with that," he said. "Meanwhile, let's all take a few hours to get some rest and meet back here again in the morning."

He watched Hayley grab her satchel, take a quick look at her phone screen and then move toward the door. He couldn't help feeling uneasy, but he couldn't force her off the case. In the long run, though, she might be safer if she stayed in the pursuit, surrounded by people looking out for her and each other. She would certainly be safer once they got Foster off the streets.

He just hoped she would survive the hunt.

"Why did you follow me here after I left your office?" Hayley asked Jack in the parking lot of the Riverside Inn. She didn't bother to keep the note of irritation out of her voice.

Jack stood beside the open door of his truck, shifting his gaze from Hayley's face to their surroundings, which he scanned for potential threats, and then back again. "I'm here because I wanted to be nearby if Foster followed you home and took another shot at you." He offered her a half smile. "I'm running short on bounty hunters right now. I can't afford to be careless with them."

"Well, thanks, I guess."

"You're welcome."

She hesitated, waiting for him to add the word *kid* to the end of his sentence. If he called her a kid again she'd punch him.

He didn't. And after a moment, she realized she was overreacting. It had been a traumatic day. Her nerves were frayed. The man wasn't intending to insult her. He just had an overall annoying personality. And he apparently thought he was funny.

Hayley had realized he was following her shortly after she left his office. She'd already decided not to return home to her empty apartment. Instead, she'd made a series of turns that took her to the road running alongside the Range River. That road had led her to the old Riverside Inn and its surrounding woodsy grounds.

Her oldest brother, Connor—half-brother, actually—had inherited the historical building from his mother and invested a substantial amount of money in fixing it up. He'd turned it into a private residence, so there were no rooms rented out to the public, but he'd offered each of his two siblings their own permanent bedroom for use whenever they wanted it. He was also generous about offering people in need, especially people in danger, a place to stay since the inn was a secure location. The Range River Bail Bonds office, where they met with bail bond applicants, was in a storefront on the other side of town.

The desire for security had sent Hayley in this direction rather than toward her apartment. Her brothers and their close family friend, Wade Fast Horse, were still out of town on a manhunt, but she'd received a text from Maribel Fast Horse letting her know that she would be staying at the inn tonight to keep an eye on the property as well as on the resident dogs and cats. The promise of company while Hayley decompressed from the day's events had been extremely appealing.

Jack lingered in the parking lot, his gaze fixed for a moment on the stone and heavy timber building behind Hayley. "Your brother has done a great job with this old place. How long has it been since the reconstruction was completed?"

"Three years." Hayley brushed her hair out of her eyes. She knew he was trying to be friendly, and she didn't want to be rude. "Did you want to have a look inside?" she asked after a moment's hesitation. She wasn't exactly in the mood to play generous hostess, but she knew a lot of people in town were curious about the inn's remodel, and she didn't want to be a jerk to him. He'd come running when she'd called for help in the Blue Mountain forest today.

"I'm sure Maribel has made something delicious for dinner," she added. Hayley had been exhausted and ravenous for the last hour, and he must be, too. "She always makes more than enough food. Come eat with us." The invitation was out of her mouth before she realized what she was saying.

Jack tilted his head slightly and gave her a slow teasing smile that sent an electrical charge zinging across the pit of her stomach.

Where had *that* feeling come from? *Seriously?* Jack Colter was, like, Connor's age. And he was *forty.* Hayley was only twenty-six. This stupid tingly feeling could not be happening. Not with a man the same age as her oldest brother. Not with a guy who, while not exactly a family enemy, was most definitely a family business rival. *The* rival for the region when it came to the bounty hunting business.

*Just stop,* she commanded herself. This was ridiculous. She didn't have those kinds of feelings—or any other kind of feelings—for

Jack Colter. She was just tired. And hungry. She was worried sick about Luther. That's all this was. Nerves and fatigue and weird residual energy at the end of a tough day.

"Thanks," Jack said in a silky voice. "Maybe another time."

Maybe another time? Wait. *What?* Did he think she was *flirting* with him, asking him on a "date"? He did! She was pretty certain he actually *did*.

Anger, embarrassment and indignation burned hot on her cheeks. And then her entire face got warm. It was probably bright red. She could only hope he didn't notice.

"Yeah, sure," she muttered. "Another time." Quite a few other responses had popped into her mind, but she'd learned long ago that when she was mad it was best to limit herself to as few words as possible until her temper cooled down. "Good night," she said abruptly, turning on her heels and practically running for the inn.

"See you in the morning," he called after her.

Yeah, great. She was going to have to see him tomorrow. And each day after until they caught Foster. She already had plenty of motivation to catch Foster, but the desire to get away from Jack and stay away from him certainly added to it. He was trouble.

She flipped up the cover on the security pad beside the front door and punched in her code. She could hear that Jack hadn't driven away yet. She knew he was watching her, waiting to make sure she got safely inside.

For some reason that made her feel edgy.

She heard the bolts on the door lock disengage. She opened it, stepped inside and then slammed it shut behind her.

Three dogs barking a happy greeting bounded toward her from the direction of the kitchen. A couple of cats slinked out from the den near the dining room to see what was going on. In front of her, flames flickered in a large fireplace flanked by floor-to-ceiling draperies. During daytime, the windows would be uncovered and offer a view of the outside deck and the Range River just beyond it.

Hayley dropped her satchel and utility belt on the couch and locked her gun in the safe in the den. Then she walked back into the high-ceilinged great room where Maribel stood there waiting for her.

"Well, I imagine you've had a rough day." Maribel offered a sympathetic smile. The raven-haired, brown-eyed woman was the mother of Range River bounty hunter Wade Fast Horse and a mother figure to the Ryan clan.

After their parents had died, Hayley and her brother Danny were raised by their older half-brother, Connor, but Maribel in their lives had been a blessing.

Eventually Maribel went to work for Connor when he started the bail bond business. She'd begun as a researcher and office manager, and then took on the duties of managing the inn property after Connor bought it.

Hayley took a deep breath and blew it out. "It has been a hard day. Harder for Luther Garcia." Earlier in the day she'd sent Maribel a text telling her what had happened.

"We'll keep him in our prayers."

"I've been praying for him all day," Hayley said, trying not to cry. Now that she was here, in the place that felt most like home to her, she could let her guard down a little.

"I've got a chicken pot pie cooling on the counter," Maribel said after giving Hayley a good, strong hug. "Let me dish some up for you. We can sit at the kitchen table and you can tell me everything."

It was hard to name the most valuable element Maribel added to the Range River team. But her willingness to sit with someone and offer an attentive ear held worth beyond measure.

"While I'm getting your food, give Connor a call. He said he wanted to speak with you as soon as you got here no matter how late it was."

Hayley had exchanged texts with him throughout the day. He was her boss as well as her brother, and she did need to talk to him. He was an excellent bounty hunter and she was anxious to hear his suggestions regarding the next steps she should take to find Foster.

After her call to Connor, and after her dinner with Maribel, Hayley intended to spend a few hours researching Foster, reviewing his bail bond files and profiling him as much as possible to help with her pursuit. And maybe get a hint on who his two companions were.

Foster wouldn't get away with hurting Luther. Not if she could do anything about it. For that matter, he wasn't walking away from trying to kill Hayley, either. Or harming anyone else. She was determined to track down the thug and the two men who were with him in the forest—whoever they were—and get them all locked up. The public would be safer. And as an added benefit, once it was all over, she would never have to work with Jack Colter again.

As she looked through the notes on Foster, her eye landed on a report by prosecutors: Foster had murdered his criminal colleague because he believed the guy had double-crossed him and deserved to be hunted and executed for his alleged misdeeds.

She inhaled sharply. The man was obsessed with seeking vengeance on those he believed had harmed him. That now included her.

# THREE

Jack walked out the door of the Blue Mountain Feed and Tack store the next morning and flipped up the collar of his jacket. The weather would be cold, soon. *Very* cold in a few weeks.

He heard Hayley walk through the feed store door behind him, politely adding her thanks to those Jack had already expressed to the store's owner when he'd been willing to listen to their questions about their fugitive. Unfortunately, he hadn't been able to give them any useful information.

"We're getting nowhere fast," Hayley muttered as she caught up with Jack and they strode side by side across the dirt parking lot, headed for his truck.

"Are you always such a downer?" Jack kept a watchful eye on their surroundings as they walked. Foster's actions had made it clear he wanted Hayley dead just about as much as he wanted his freedom. So that meant there was a good chance that the fugitive had not only hunkered down in town or nearby, but that he could also come out of hiding at any time to take another shot at Hayley.

He glanced over at her. Hayley's face muscles looked tense, she had dark circles under her eyes and she was also scanning their surroundings.

He couldn't blame her for being nervous.

"No wonder Range River Bail Bonds is second to my Eagle Rapids Bail Bonds." Jack continued his banter, hoping to lighten her mood. Her life was in danger and she needed to be vigilant, but that didn't mean she had to be miserable. "Y'all need an attitude adjustment if you want to fly high like us."

*"Excuse me?"* Hayley turned to glare at him.

"Every bit of information is useful when you're tracking somebody." Jack kept going, intentionally adopting a haughty, patronizing tone just to make things interesting. "Searching for someone in a location and finding they're not there is useful information. Asking someone—like the guy at the feed store—if they've seen someone around town or in the nearby neighborhoods, and having them tell you that they *haven't*, is helpful. It lets you cross things off your list of possibilities."

He was curious to see if she took offense at his goading and lost her temper, because that would give him important information about her.

Jack needed to know precisely what kind of personality he was working with and he needed that information quickly. They were wading deeper into what looked like a tougher, more dangerous job than he'd imagined at the start, especially now that Hayley was a target. Staying in control, especially when being intentionally goaded by someone acting like a jerk, was a tough skill to learn. It usually took time and maturity.

Hayley was only twenty-six.

There was quite a difference in age between them. Something he needed to keep in mind. Because he realized he enjoyed being in her company and teasing her just a little too much.

Not that he was looking for a romantic partner. Hadn't been for a long time.

As they climbed into his truck, he prepared himself for a verbal blasting in response to his intentionally annoying comments.

He started up the engine. After maybe thirty seconds of unexpected silence he turned to her, anticipating a red-faced, frowning bounty hunter ready to hold forth on how he'd unforgivably insulted her and her family business.

Instead, he saw the easy posture of a woman without a care in the world. Her arms were at her sides instead of defensively crossed over her chest. Her shoulders looked calm and relaxed instead of tensed and ready for a fight. However, the smile on her lips didn't quite reach her dark blue eyes, which looked like they were shooting sparks in his direction.

"My brother Connor raised me from the time I was seven years old and he's always emphasized the importance of a good attitude," she said sweetly. "I'm so happy to know that *you* were finally able to grasp the concept. Better late than never."

Jack laughed. Couldn't help it. Hayley was sharp, not easily manipulated, and knowing that made him feel better about their chances of keeping her alive while hunting for Foster and his accomplices.

"The park where Foster shot at me is at the end of this street," Hayley said, directing the conversation back to the business at hand.

"He vanished quickly, which tells us he's familiar with the area. Since the cops haven't picked him up on the highway or tracked him to another location through his credit card or cell phone use, I think there's a reasonable chance he's still in town. That feed store was the fifth place we've stopped at this morning where no one could tell us anything about him or the two other men who were with him. Somebody *must* have seen something useful. They're just refusing to talk to us about it."

"People are afraid," Jack said as he pulled out onto the road. "He's already murdered two people, plus he put Luther in Intensive Care, and he tried to kill you. I'm not surprised people don't want to get involved."

The bounty hunting crew had met at his Range River office early this morning. He'd had a brief phone conversation with Luther's wife and learned that Luther was still unconscious and not doing any better. The plan for today was for Milo and Katherine to work out of the office, placing calls to Foster's family members and known associates. They would also contact confidential informants across the region and put out the word that there was reward money available for information on Foster's whereabouts.

Law enforcement had access to resources far beyond what the bail bond companies could possibly have. They were good at what they did and a large percentage of the time the cops got results. But sometimes bad guys on the run were able to shake them off.

That left room for resourceful bounty hunters to step in. They had a network of informants to help them, but beyond that they were able to obtain information from people who for various reasons were not willing to talk to the cops. Or from people the police had simply never crossed paths with.

"I know the citizens of Blue Mountain are scared to help catch these thugs," Hayley said as they drove down the road. "I would be, too, if I didn't have training, a weapon and colleagues to back me up. But staying out of the pursuit doesn't necessarily keep them safe from danger. If Foster takes another shot at me—or the police, or anyone else—one of the town's residents could get hit in the crossfire."

Jack glanced at her. "I'd prefer it if we could prevent a situation where he shoots at you again."

"I'll do my best to stay out of the line of fire, but I can't promise anything."

He couldn't ask for more than that. It was the nature of the business,

They drove around aimlessly for a few minutes, heading up and down several residential streets in town, both of them on the lookout for anything that seemed "off"— broken windows or doors indicating a burglary—but nothing popped. So he steered toward the highway, and then doubled back. When Hayley gave him a questioning look, he explained, "I don't want a tail, and I don't want anybody giving away our whereabouts unintentionally."

Eventually Jack parked outside a corner coffee shop. They went inside with photos of Foster and hopes that someone had seen him around, or maybe had seen the bad guys fleeing after the shootings yesterday. The woman at the cash register was a definite *no* on a sighting, and so was the short-order cook. But a waitress and busboy exchanged glances at their questioning, and Jack approached them and showed them the photos.

"No, sorry," the waitress said without giving the pictures more than a blink, while the busboy stared at his sneakers.

"Is that sorry, you didn't see him or sorry, you don't want to tell us you saw him?" Hayley said, her voice cold as steel. She turned to the busboy. "What about you?"

"Nah, looks like about a dozen fellows who come in here. Can't tell one from the other." He hurried off, as if his life depended on clearing the next table.

Jack faced the waitress. "If your memory improves, give us a call." He handed her a card. "I'd think really hard, if I were you. These men won't hesitate to kill again, and you don't want to be the one who could have stopped them."

When they walked out of the coffee shop, a police cruiser pulled to the curb and Officer Cal Parker waved them over and asked if they'd learned anything. The Blue Mountain police chief, Rafael Silva, was okay with the bounty hunters' help up to a point, which made things a little easier. Local police didn't always welcome bounty hunters with open arms, as was evidenced by Officer Parker's snappish attitude when they had a brief conversation with him before he drove off.

Jack and Hayley headed back to the truck. They could visit a few more businesses in the area, but Jack figured that wasn't the best use of their time. They'd probably get the same results that they'd been getting all morning.

For the last hour or so he'd been pondering a different tactic. And he'd finally decided it was a good idea. The two of them could hide the fact that they were bounty hunters and go undercover as husband and wife. That might make people more willing to talk to them.

It was a reasonable idea. And it wasn't as if Jack had a wife or girlfriend who could hear about the subterfuge and feel threatened. He was unattached and determined to stay that way.

He'd tied the knot when he was young, shortly after he'd enlisted in the army. But once he deployed overseas, his twenty-year-old wife realized that she couldn't tolerate so much time on her own. She'd concluded their marriage was a mistake, filed for divorce and that was that.

Hayley might be six years older than his wife had been when they'd gotten married, but even twenty-six seemed young to a man in his forties. Too young to realize the depth of commitment it took to sustain a marriage. Not that it mattered. Not that Hayley's depth of character—or lack thereof—was even any of Jack's business.

He didn't intend to take that kind of emotional risk ever again, no matter how appealing the woman was.

"What do you want to do next?" Hayley asked after they were back inside the truck with their seat belts fastened.

Jack started up the engine and then turned to her. "Let's get married."

# FOUR

For a moment, Hayley was sure she'd misheard him.

Then, when she realized she hadn't, her stomach did an odd little lurch. Like a trout doing a quicksilver jump out of the water. It wasn't an unpleasant feeling, but it was…well, it was *something*.

She didn't realize her mouth was hanging open in surprise until Jack reached over, placed two fingers under her chin and gently closed it for her.

His touch, coupled with the smirk on his lips, snapped her attention back into focus.

"Why would I marry *you*?" She immediately regretted the tone of her response. The man wanted to get under her skin and she'd just confirmed his success.

She quickly composed herself, determined

to ignore the weird flash of emotions he'd drawn out of her with his stupid proposal.

"I'm talking a *pretend* marriage," Jack added, with one eyebrow lifted and the hint of a smile on his lips. "I thought that was obvious. We could go undercover as a married couple who are considering a permanent move to the area. Together with Milo and Katherine, we could rent a cabin near the lake for a couple of nights."

"How do you figure that's going to speed up the hunt for Foster and his thug friends?" Hayley wasn't comfortable with lying to people or misrepresenting who she was, but sometimes going undercover was the only way to capture the bad guys.

"If we get rid of our utility belts, dress a little more casually and just mosey around the lake and the nearby park and campground for a couple of days, maybe some of the outdoorsy people will talk with us. It's the kind of setting where people are a little more inclined to be chatty with strangers."

Hayley took a quick glance out the window, considering the idea. "Well, I'd say most of the business owners right around here know we're bounty hunters. And they definitely aren't anxious to give us any information."

"Right. So now we lean in a different direction."

"How so, exactly?"

"The shooting in the town park yesterday has hit the news. Foster's picture has popped up on TV and online. So maybe we could strike up a casual conversation about that with people. See what they say. It's not a big town, but our photos weren't in the story. Nothing about us was, really."

"We might come across someone who spotted Foster driving a vehicle they could describe to us, or a boat," Hayley mused aloud. "He could have been staying at the campground by the lake and maybe somebody saw him there. We know he hasn't been staying in a hotel or the police would have found him by now."

"Right." Jack nodded. "Even if he's moved on, the details of where he *has* been could give us some clues on how to find him now."

"That's actually a good idea." Hayley eyed him, wondering how long she could take being practically glued to his side pretending to be his wife. She already felt like the interior of his truck was way too small and they were sitting way too close together.

"How long did you want to do this?"

"A couple days."

Hayley didn't have any better ideas. "Okay," she said. "Let's do it. But first we need to make a quick trip back to Range River so I can grab some clothes."

Jack placed a call to Milo, who confirmed that he and Katherine were agreeable to the plan.

He disconnected and then pulled out into the street. At the first stoplight they came to, Hayley glanced over at him. He was smiling at her.

"What?" she demanded.

"I'm just happy that when I asked you to marry me, you finally said yes."

She felt her cheeks get warm. She hoped they weren't red. They probably were.

Jack laughed. The delighted sound seemed incongruous with the sharp angles of his face and the serious expression in his eyes.

Hayley found herself laughing with him despite her intention not to.

A few minutes later, the smile on her lips fell away as they passed the town park and then the stretch of forest near where she and Luther had been attacked. Knots of anxiety forced their way back into her abdomen, twisting it until she felt a slight ache.

They *had* to get Foster and his criminal companions before they could hurt anyone else. And before the fugitive could target Hayley again.

That was reason enough for her to go through with a fake marriage to Jack. She could take it. It would only be for a couple of days.

The town of Blue Mountain sprawled along the edges of Peregrine Lake. The body of cool, deep water was one of the main draws for people heading to the town for a visit.

Standing at the lake's shoreline, Hayley gazed at the azure water. The surface rippled under a cool breeze. The bounty hunters had made short work of the trip to Range River and back. Together with Milo and Katherine, Hayley and Jack had rented a vacation cabin near the lake's edge where they'd dropped off their bags.

Milo and Katherine had headed into the nearby campground to try and strike up friendly conversations that might lead to useful information.

Hayley and Jack were at the lakeside area and adjoining park where they'd already chatted with several people. So far, neither team had learned anything helpful.

"I'm starting to feel like we're wasting time on this." Hayley turned to Jack.

Guilt over what had happened to Luther had crept back into her consciousness and it was making her frustrated.

"I'm not normally so impatient," she muttered. Her job often required her to watch and wait for long periods of time and she was usually self-disciplined enough to do it without complaint. What they were doing wasn't exactly sitting and waiting, but it was starting to feel like it.

"It's the guilt over Luther pushing you," Jack said, seeming to read her thoughts. "I know what that's like."

Maybe he had been through something similar. But her guilt was combined with a lifelong compulsion to prove to her brothers that she was worthy of the sacrifices they'd made to help raise her after their parents died.

That drive to make her brothers proud of her was the reason why she had to be *the* bounty hunter who slapped handcuffs on Barry Foster. Him *and* his two loser companions, if possible. She wanted to show her family—including Maribel and Wade Fast Horse—how much she loved and appreciated them. And she could do that by making sure Range River Bail Bonds got credit for this high-profile fugitive recovery.

Jack Colter and his Eagle Rapids Bail Bonds team could catch the next fugitive they chased.

This capture *had* to be hers. For the sake of her family. And for Luther.

But giving in to impatience was not going to help.

She took a deep breath and blew it out. *Lord, please help me to keep my thoughts and priorities straight.*

She didn't feel much different in the next moment. But she would do the right thing and hope that the feeling of balance she needed would eventually follow.

"You're right," she said to Jack, practically choking on the words. The acknowledgment would likely puff up his already inflated ego. "Your plan is a good one. Let's stick with it a little longer."

She braced herself for his gloating response.

Instead of a grin or a wink, he simply gave her a quick nod acknowledging that he'd heard her. Then he reached for her hand.

It was a big hand. Strong and slightly calloused. Hayley's heart sped up a little. Jack took a step forward while she remained rooted to the spot, appalled by the rush of emotion roiling through her.

"We're supposed to look like we're married," Jack said. "Holding hands while we walk around might help sell the idea."

"Of course." Hayley's emotions were getting even more tangled and confusing. She was attracted to Jack even though she didn't want to be.

She fell in step beside him as they headed for the boardwalk alongside a section of the lake's edge.

"Let's head for the hamburger stand," Hayley said. "People like to sit at the outside tables. Maybe we'll find somebody there who has useful information."

They ordered sandwiches and sodas at the take-out window and then sat down at a rickety round table that Jack dragged toward a juncture between two buildings. Positioned there, with walls on two sides, meant that Hayley wasn't such an easy target should Barry Foster have his sites trained on her. Thick stands of tall pine trees surrounded the lake's edge and Foster could be hidden behind one of those trees right now, watching Hayley. If he had a rifle, taking her out would be an easy shot.

With her mind lingering on that thought, Hayley found it hard to enjoy her food. She forced down a few bites for the sake of maintaining her energy, but then gave up and just sipped her soda. After they finished eating, they walked around and chatted with a few people, but they didn't have as much of an opportunity to gather information as they'd hoped. The early-evening breeze, while not strong, was steady. And cold. There weren't that many people out. Winter would make a dramatic snowy appearance before too long.

"Maybe there will be a bigger crowd out here tomorrow morning," Jack said as the boardwalk shops started closing down. "The diehard fishermen and women will be up early. All we'll have to do is ask them what's biting and that'll get them talking. And then we can shift the conversation toward Foster. Let's turn in early so we can be back out here by sunrise."

"Okay. I'll text Katherine and let her know what we're doing."

A short time later, all four bounty hunters were back at the cabin where they made their plans for the following day. When that was done, Jack called Jessica Garcia and learned that Luther had developed a fever and was not doing well. With Luther's wife still on the phone, the bounty hunters joined her in prayer for him.

"It's going to be a chilly night," Milo said after the phone call ended. He lit the potbellied pellet stove in the living room.

The warmth radiating from the stove was soothing, and after Hayley sent a text to Connor summarizing the day's events, she finally found herself able to relax somewhat. She hadn't slept well last night, waking up every hour, it seemed. Maybe tonight she would be able to catch up on her rest.

Everyone seemed ready to turn in early.

Milo and Katherine settled into the upstairs bedroom. Hayley took the downstairs bedroom while Jack volunteered to sleep on the very uncomfortable-looking bed that pulled out from the couch in the living room.

After wishing everyone a good night, Hayley went into her room, closed the door and dropped down onto the bed. She'd change into her T-shirt and sweatpants later. Right now she just wanted to rest for a minute.

But as soon as she closed her eyes, in her mind she could see Barry Foster's face and that malicious smile. She shook her head, trying to shake off the image. She'd thought about him all day today. If she thought about him now, she'd never get any sleep. And if she were exhausted, she wouldn't be able to track him down and throw him in jail tomorrow.

Determined to turn her thoughts away

from him, she began to think of verses from her favorite Psalms, and she started to pray.

She must have fallen asleep, because suddenly she was jolted out of a dream about an Independence Day celebration and fireworks. She had also been dreaming about smoke.

No, wait, she *smelled* smoke. For real. Not in a dream.

Vaguely, she wondered if it was coming from the pellet stove in the living room. Maybe the flue needed cleaning.

*"Fire! Everybody out!"*

Jack threw open her door, yelled at her to get outside and then turned and ran up the narrow staircase to alert Milo and Katherine.

Hayley heard them opening their door before Jack made it to the top of the stairs.

Her shoes were still on, so she leaped off the bed, grabbed her phone and her satchel and started punching in a call to 9-1-1.

The smoke was getting thick. She reached the living room and saw the orange glow of fire. The others clambered down the stairs behind her as she raced to the cabin's entrance.

She unbolted the door, threw it open and was met with a barrage of gunfire.

# FIVE

Jack raced down the final few steps of the cabin's narrow staircase and sprinted toward the front door. The smoke pouring out of the small kitchen and into the living room was rapidly gaining volume. "Hayley!"

The sound of gunfire had sent his heart hammering in fear for her safety.

"Here!" she called out in response.

He could see now that she'd slammed the front door closed, flipped the heavy wooden coffee table onto its side to form a barricade and then taken cover behind it with her handgun drawn and pointed toward the door.

Jack dropped down beside her.

"I didn't know if whoever was out there would try to rush in after they stopped shooting," Hayley said, sounding out of breath.

"Good call."

"Figured I'd stay right here for a minute

or two until I knew what was happening," she added.

Jack looked around. They were trapped, that much was certain. The only other door out of the cabin was in the kitchen where the fire had started. They were going to have to break a window to escape.

"What happened?" Hayley demanded. "How did the fire start?"

"Two Molotov cocktails flung through the kitchen window." The hot, ashy smoke burned his lungs as he drew in a breath to speak.

"I ran in there thinking I could put them out, but one of them had exploded on the counter and already set the curtains on fire. The flames reached the wooden cupboards before I could do anything. The other exploded on the rug in front of the sink, lit it up, and then the fire moved into the floorboards. It was moving too fast for me to put it out."

"And now Foster and his friends are waiting outside to shoot us when we can't stand the heat and smoke any longer and we have to get out." Hayley turned toward to the door. "It's got to be them. Who else would it be?"

Katherine and Milo hit the bottom of the stairs. Katherine was already on speakerphone with an emergency operator, calmly but urgently describing the situation. She and her husband stayed low as they moved into the living room.

There was a quick series of sparking and buzzing sounds, and then the lights throughout the cabin went out.

The only illumination was a small rectangle of light from Katherine's phone and the glow from the fire.

The room was heating up, fast. The air felt depleted of oxygen and Jack realized he was getting light-headed. "We have to get outside, *now.*"

"There hasn't been any more gunfire," Hayley said in a scratchy voice.

"Maybe the shooter—or shooters—have backed off to avoid getting caught. They must know we've called 9-1-1 by now and that firefighters and cops are on the way."

The ceiling began to make creaking and groaning sounds. The heat was radiating upward toward the second story, with accompanying flames possibly traveling through the walls.

The building could collapse on them at any moment.

Jack looked toward the front door. Did they dare make a run for it through that door or try to slip out through the large window beside it? There was only one other possible exit available to them. A small window in the bedroom where Hayley had been sleeping. But what if Foster or one of his pals were waiting outside that window ready to finish them off as they tried to escape?

"You got an ETA on fire or cops or *anybody* that could help us?" Hayley hollered to Katherine.

Katherine repeated the question into her phone, her voice strained with tension as she shouted to be heard over the noises made by the burning building.

"Operator says they're almost here," Katherine called out.

Katherine and her husband were volunteer firefighters. But their training and experience weren't of much use without their gear.

Something collapsed in the kitchen—maybe a section of wall, it was hard to tell through the smoke—and a scorching burst of heat rushed into the living room.

"We can't wait for help any longer," Hayley said. "We have to get out now."

Escape through the front door or by way

of the bedroom window. Either option could be a fatal decision ending in gunfire.

But they had to do *something*.

"They'll expect us to try to escape through the bedroom window," Jack answered her. "That's how they set this up. That's what they want us to do. I think that's most likely where they're waiting."

Hayley nodded.

"I'm going out through the front door." Jack said it loud enough for Katherine and Milo to hear. "If somebody's out there and they start shooting, I'll draw their gunfire away from the cabin. The rest of you rush out behind me as soon as it's safe and run for cover as fast as you can."

"Jack, I don't think—" Milo started to speak, but Jack interrupted him.

"If you've got a better plan, what is it?" he demanded.

Milo stared at him wordlessly.

Jack got up from behind the coffee table barricade and moved toward the front door with its pattern of scattered bullet holes. Gun in hand, he unfastened the latch. Then he crouched down and stayed behind the door, using it as a flimsy barrier as he slowly pulled it open.

The initial rush of cool, fresh air gave him such a feeling of relief that his knees nearly buckled.

He waited for a moment, listening for sounds of bad guys out in front of the cabin. He didn't hear anything, so he started to move. He was around the edge of the door, nearly to the threshold, when he heard a first shot that struck the doorjamb and sent large splinters of wood flying.

More shots followed in rapid succession, forcing Jack to duck back into the house. He slammed the door shut and moved away as fast as he could. The others, who had moved forward when he opened the door, also moved back to where they'd been before.

*Now what?*

The heat from the fire was nearly unbearable.

"We have to at least *try* to get out through the bedroom window. We've got no other choice," Hayley said. "This time I'll go first."

He couldn't let her do it. The first one out would be the most vulnerable to getting shot.

"You're working on *my* team," Jack said. "*I* make the decisions."

"You can believe that if you want to," Hayley said.

Jack was more stunned than angry. People just didn't talk to him like that.

He followed her to the bedroom where she grabbed a small bedside table and swung it to break the glass.

As he feared, her efforts were greeted with gunfire.

They both hit the ground.

Forcing himself to stay calm and *think*, Jack was trying to drum up other possible options when he heard a banging sound.

Was someone pounding on the front door?

The banging continued.

It was coming from inside the house, toward the living room, near the bottom of the stairs.

He glanced over and locked eyes with Hayley. She'd obviously heard it, too.

Staying low they crawled into the living room where they saw Katherine on her back, kicking her heel at the wall. "I saw a fire-fighting training video once—didn't think of it until now—that showed how you can sometimes kick your way through wooden planks or drywall and make your way out if you get trapped."

Sure enough, with the next kick she put a hole through a wooden plank between two widely spaced supporting boards.

Hayley kept an eye on the front door in case thugs tried to open it and shoot at them again while Katherine, Milo and Jack kicked at the drywall and planks underneath until they'd cleared enough space for a person to pass through.

Jack stuck his head out. He didn't see the assailants, so with his gun in his hand he crawled the rest of the way through.

For the first few seconds he lay on the cool, damp grass, gulping clear air and scanning the area around him.

There was no one in sight.

He turned and gestured at Hayley to climb the rest of the way out. With weapons drawn, the two of them crouched on the ground and provided cover while Katherine and then Milo also escaped the burning cabin.

For the first few moments, all any of them did was breathe.

Away from the sounds of the fire and the slowly collapsing cabin, Jack heard the wail of approaching sirens. The bounty hunters were at the back corner of the cabin, facing the woods, but he could see flashes of blue and red light washing across the tall pine trees as the emergency responders pulled up in front of the cabin.

"The cavalry is here," Milo said wearily. "Yay."

"Our bad guys might be lurking nearby watching everything," Hayley said to Jack.

He nodded. "Let's take a look around."

Still coughing and wheezing a little, they conducted a quick search in the shadows around the burning cabin as well as around a couple of nearby cabins.

The only people they came across were innocent neighbors huddled outside their residences, watching the firefighters working to extinguish the blaze.

Jack tried not to give in to the heavy feeling of disappointment that settled over him as he had to admit that the assailants had gotten away.

"I didn't see the shooter or shooters, either," Hayley said to Blue Mountain Police Chief Rafael Silva as she stood across from him on the narrow road in front of the partially collapsed cabin. Officer Parker stood beside the chief, while Jack stayed by Hayley's side.

The fire had been extinguished and the firefighting crew was now inside the cabin raking through the debris and looking for potential hidden hotspots.

Jack had given his statement first and now Hayley was wrapping up her turn at describing what she'd experienced. Katherine and Milo, since they had previously trained with some of the local firefighters and were known to them, had been loaned some personal protective gear so they could go back inside the cabin and look for the bounty hunters' personal belongings. "I didn't have the front door open all the way when the first round of shots started," Hayley continued. "The porchlight was on, but it only illuminated a small area. Beyond that it was dark. So I didn't see anything. Not a person. Not a car or truck. Nothing."

She'd already mentally kicked herself for not making the extra effort to spot the shooter or a vehicle before she'd slammed the door shut.

"Even though I didn't see them, I'm sure Barry Foster and his two thug friends were responsible for this. There's no one else who would have a motive to come after us like this," she added.

A fire captain stepped out of the cabin and

made a beckoning gesture toward the police chief.

"Excuse me," Silva said. He started to walk away and then stopped and turned. "Don't head back home to Range River just yet. I might want to talk to you again later tonight."

"Of course," Hayley said.

Jack voiced his agreement, as well.

"Keep an eye on the perimeter of the scene," Silva said to Parker. "We all know how firebugs often like to hang around to see the results of their handiwork. Maybe that will be the case with this." He turned and resumed his walk toward the fire captain.

Hayley glanced up and down the street, wondering if the firebombing criminals really were nearby and watching.

Foster was definitely after *her*, personally, for some reason.

His irrational behavior scared her. She'd experienced lots of criminals using every threat, weapon and form of attack they could think of to try to frighten her off the chase when she was hunting them. But having a fugitive go to the extremes Foster was going to and actually track her down and try to kill her was something she'd never faced before. And she wasn't sure how to handle it.

*Dear Lord, please give me the wisdom I need right now.*

She tilted her head back to gaze at the night sky, sighed deeply and worked to calm her emotions and focus her thoughts.

The thing that gnawed at her the most was the fact that she was putting Jack and his bounty hunters in serious danger by working alongside them. The job had its risks, of course. Everybody in the profession knew that. But this was beyond the norm. Maybe unreasonably so. Perhaps it was time for her to break away from them and make the capture on her own.

Jack moved closer to her, laid a hand on her shoulder and gave it a gentle, lingering squeeze. "We'll get them."

"*We* will get whoever did this," Officer Parker interjected. "The police, *not* bounty hunters, will deal with this crime and any other crimes Foster and his criminal friends commit in this town."

Hayley looked over at the blond cop. *Somebody* apparently felt like his toes were being stepped on. This wasn't the first time Hayley had come across an attitude like this from a law officer. It probably wouldn't be the last time, either.

"Of course it's the job of the police to handle this crime," she responded. She was a bounty hunter, not a cop. And not a vigilante.

She stole a quick glance at Jack to see his reaction. The reputation that preceded him had her expecting that he would balk at the suggestion he place limits on how far he would go to capture their fugitive. But he didn't.

He simply removed his hand from Hayley's shoulder and nodded at Parker.

"I understand why you're inclined to assume Foster is behind this," the officer said. "There's a good chance you're right. Nevertheless, solving crimes is *not* your job. Investigating them and assigning blame is not your job. Apprehending your bail jumper— for whom an arrest warrant has been issued— is the *only* action you are authorized to take."

"Agreed," Hayley said, itching to tell the guy she'd gotten his message the first time he'd said it.

Afraid that she'd give in to the urge to make a less-than-diplomatic comment, she turned her attention back to the scorched cabin, visible in the illumination cast by the headlights of the fire engines. There was a slight haze from the residual smoke in the air, but the breeze seemed to be moving it out pretty quickly.

A couple of county deputy sheriff patrol units had responded to the scene. They'd requested a K-9 to help search the area for suspects or maybe get an indication of which direction they'd fled. But the county only had two K-9 officers, with the nearest stationed in Range River. So it was taking time for the officer and her dog to respond.

A scattering of nearby residents and some people staying at the campground had wandered over to watch when the fire was at its height. The cops had spoken with them, trying to find out if anyone had witnessed the initial attack or the shootings. None of them had seen anything other than the fire, which was what had drawn them over. Now that the drama had wound down, they'd all left.

Parker got a summons over his radio and walked away while speaking into his collar mic.

"What do you want to do next?" Jack asked as soon as the officer was out of earshot.

Hayley's stomach clenched. Maybe this was the moment when Jack would demonstrate his tendency to work outside the guidelines Parker had emphasized. The thought made her nervous, because she was so angry and so determined to capture Foster and his companions that she feared she would be tempted to cross the line right alongside him.

"Did you have any ideas you want to suggest?" she asked cautiously.

He hooked a thumb in the direction of the lake, little more than a mile away. "I know it's getting late, but it *is* a Saturday night. Why don't we go mill around and see who's still out and about at the campground or the park? Everybody over there must have heard the sirens. They probably all smelled the smoke, too. And they must have seen the glow from the fire if not the actual flames. Who knows? Maybe the lookie-loos who were here earlier will have a different story to tell when there aren't any cops around."

"Are you thinking we'll go ahead and identify ourselves as bounty hunters?"

"Nope. I'm not ready to give up on our *marriage*." He offered her a half grin. "I say we go back to our married couple checking out the town act. Strike up some conversations. Right now we could ask some pretty direct questions about Foster and crime and anything anyone might have heard or seen tonight or last night near the park shooting.

Those kinds of questions might make people suspicious under normal circumstances, but with the fire tonight and the police presence, it could actually seem normal."

"That's not such a bad idea." She couldn't resist teasing him a little. They were competitors, and she would not forget that. But she'd seen for herself that he put his concerns for his team over himself and fears for his own safety. Which didn't exactly fit the rumors she'd heard about him. They were never going to be friends. After this manhunt was over, they'd go their separate ways. But in the meantime, maybe she could lighten up just a little. They were both experiencing enough stress from the manhunt and the attacks. Why add to it?

Jack winked at her. "Thanks for the vote of confidence."

"We just need to be especially cautious while we're around the campers. I don't want anybody getting hurt if Foster tries again to come after me tonight."

Jack captured her gaze and held it. "We'll be careful. And he's not going to get you. I'm not going to let that happen."

The warmth in his eyes held her transfixed for a moment. And then, with a slight shiver, she came to her senses. "You don't let humility get in your way too often, do you?"

He grinned. "I know you're competent and can take care of yourself. I just want you to know I've got your back."

His tone was light, but his message was serious. She knew he'd try to protect her if he could, but she was coming to the conclusion that she might protect him best if she wasn't part of the group. That thought pierced her more than she liked. She was growing fond of him. Too fond.

"Are you sure you still want me on your team after all of this?" Hayley asked. "If you and the others work on your own, you won't have to keep looking over your shoulders. You could hunt faster." And maybe safer, since Foster was targeting her.

"Are you scared to keep going?" Jack asked, taking a step closer to her. "Because if you are and you want to drop out of this manhunt, that's fine. I wouldn't blame you. You've been through a lot. Go ahead and move on to another case. And while you're working that, my crew and I will find Foster and his jerk friends."

"You want me to quit so you can make this capture."

He shrugged. "If you're going to hand Eagle Rapids Bail Bonds the win on this fugitive recovery, we're going to take it. It'll just add a little extra shine to our already stellar reputation."

There was enough light spilling over from the fire engines that she could see the challenge in his blue eyes. There was no way she could miss the cocky tilt of his head, the borderline arrogant expression on his admittedly handsome, rugged face.

She absolutely did *not* want to hand this capture over to him. No way.

What she wanted—no, what she *needed*—was to be able to look her brother Connor in the eye and tell him she'd made this capture for the Range River Bail Bonds team. For the Ryan *family* team. Wade and Maribel Fast Horse included.

"Now that I think about it, I wouldn't feel right leaving this chase when there are still so many bounty hunting techniques you're lacking that I could help you with," she said sweetly, mimicking the cocky tilt of his head.

"You think I need your help?" Jack stepped even closer to her, his gaze sharpening, a slight smile lifting the corners of his lips.

She swallowed thickly and nodded. He was

close enough now that she could feel his body heat. Despite the warmth, she shivered.

"Maybe we should help each other," Jack said. "And keep working together. My team and I can handle the danger."

"If you're sure."

He nodded. "I am. And I guarantee you Katherine and Milo would speak up if they didn't want to work with you any longer."

"Okay."

He rubbed his hands together. "Now that we've gotten that out of the way, let's drive over to the campground."

They got into his truck, where Jack paused long enough to send Milo a text letting him know where they were headed.

As Jack had predicted, there were a fair number of people milling around the campground and its adjacent park. Several small groups, many of them comprised of families with children, gathered around campfires outside their tents or trailers.

Jack wrapped a muscular arm around Hayley's shoulder as they reached the first friendly looking group. She knew he was only doing it to sell the image of them as a married couple, but his touch triggered a rush of warmth and a thrilling feeling in the pit of her stomach, nevertheless. She didn't want to give in to the wave of emotion it stirred up, but she couldn't make the feeling stop. As he spoke to the campers, and referred to her as his wife, she felt her face flush. Her brain told her that her reaction was ridiculous, but she couldn't help it.

Jack was as old as Connor, she reminded herself. He had an unsavory reputation in the bounty hunting community, he was her competition and he was *annoying*.

That he was also…well, maybe a little bit attractive and a little bit charming when he wanted to be was inconvenient, to say the least.

The people in the first group they stepped up to appeared relaxed, as if they were enjoying themselves and were willing to engage in conversation. They also seemed nervously fascinated about the Foster shooting but they had no firsthand information to offer.

Hayley and Jack got the same results with their next several attempts to chat casually with people.

They'd been making their way around the campground for a couple of hours when they came across a group of campers and spoke with one guy who mentioned having noticed something when they brought up the topic of fugitive Barry Foster.

"When my wife and kids and I first rolled into town, we stopped at that old general store, Bennie Mac's, to buy fishing licenses. Three guys were standing together in there looking at the tent displays. I remember them because one of them was wearing khakis and a dress shirt and I wondered if, like me, he'd just gotten off work and was looking to get outdoors for a bit. I thought about that when the cops were looking for that Foster guy plus a couple of other shooters who might be traveling with him."

"Did the man you're talking about look like the picture of Barry Foster that's been in the online news stories?" Hayley prompted. That *had* to be Foster and his two cronies the guy had seen. As soon as he described the shopper's clothing, she was sure of it.

The camper's face changed as soon as Hayley pressed him. He settled back and crossed his arms over his chest. She knew from his body language what was coming next. It would be a retreat.

"The picture online shows Foster as a dude with a thick head of reddish hair and a heavy beard," the camper said. "The man I saw was bald and clean-shaven. It wasn't the same guy."

"Did you report any of this to the police?" Jack asked.

The camper glanced at an adolescent girl in a camping chair, and then returned his gaze to Jack. "No, I didn't contact the cops. Because, like I said, I'm sure it wasn't Foster."

Hayley figured what he was really sure of was that he didn't want to risk putting that girl—likely his daughter—in danger. She couldn't blame him.

"We need to let Chief Silva know about this," Hayley said to Jack as soon as they walked away. "Maybe Foster bought something at Bennie Mac's and left a payment trail. Or maybe a surveillance camera caught an image of whatever vehicle he's using now."

"I know Bennie Mac's grandson," Jack said. "He runs the store. His name's Drew MacAllen. I'm sure if he's got any helpful information he'll share it with us."

While Jack's comment sounded straightforward enough, it also made Hayley nervous. She suspected that he intended to obtain bits of information from his friend that weren't shared with the police so that Jack could make the capture. For a bounty hunter, knowingly withholding significant information related to an active police investigation would be unethical and potentially illegal. Would Jack do it? His reputation would indicate that he might.

Not only did Hayley need to capture a fugitive—and hopefully his murderous thug friends at the same time—but she also needed to make sure her partner didn't use questionable man-hunting techniques that could ultimately cause *her* to lose her bounty hunting license since she was working alongside him.

And she needed to keep herself and her three fellow bounty hunters from getting killed in the process.

# SIX

"I wish citizens would come forth and report information like this." Chief Silva leaned back in his desk chair and ran a hand through his black hair.

It was closing in on two o'clock in the morning. Jack and Hayley were sitting in visitor chairs in the chief's office along with Katherine and Milo, with Officer Parker there, as well.

"The man's fear for his family's safety is real. You could see it on his face." Jack couldn't help thinking about how he would have reacted if he were in the camper's position and had a young daughter. If he were still married he could have had a daughter that age right now. Or a son. He had once hoped to have several children.

"This effort to find Foster and his cronies is definitely the kind of situation where bounty hunters can help out local police," Hayley said to Silva. "Locals might know the cops, but they won't know us." She was working hard to sell the idea of them assisting the police in some capacity so they could stay on top of information related to the Foster manhunt and connected crimes. He had to give her credit for that.

"As far as anybody can tell we're just regular people. A husband and wife visiting the area. They'd feel comfortable talking to us."

*Husband and wife.* Just hearing her use those terms made Jack's stomach twinge. Even though the pretend marriage had been his idea. The notion had seemed useful and harmless enough at the start. It was still useful. But the harmless part had changed to something more...murky.

Officer Parker, looking none too happy about the direction the conversation was going, stood in the doorway. Whether the guy really had a problem with bounty hunters specifically, or he was just a person who was constantly in a bad mood, Jack couldn't tell. It didn't really matter. Jack would stay on the hunt for Foster whether Parker liked it or not.

Around midnight Silva had finally wrapped

up the scene at the cabin fire, gotten his forensic evidence collected, sent his small police force out to scour the town searching for the bad guys and contacted the highway patrol and other local police departments to be on the lookout for Foster and his accomplices possibly fleeing the area. The sheriff's department K-9 had picked up a couple of scent trails that started out showing promise, only for them to end at the edge of the road where the assailants had presumably gotten into a vehicle and driven away.

With all of that out of the way, Silva had summoned the bounty hunters to the police department to repeat their stories and ask if they remembered any new details. Following that, Jack had told the chief about what they'd learned from the man at the campground. That Foster likely spent some time shopping at a store in town where he may have inadvertently left behind clues on where or how to find him.

"It is officially Sunday," the chief said, glancing at his computer screen. "Drew won't open the doors at Bennie Mac's General Store until eleven. I'll head over there by ten-thirty, ask him to let me in while he's having his coffee and setting things up. See what kind of information he can give me. And press him on why *he* didn't report a possible sighting of Foster."

Hayley turned to look at Jack. She raised her eyebrows and tilted her head slightly in the direction of the chief. Jack was fairly certain she was indicating she thought he should mention his connection with Drew to Silva. She was worried he would do something unethical, by hiding his knowledge of the man.

"I've worked with Drew in the past," Jack said. "He's been willing to help."

Silva nodded. "Yeah, I'm sure he'll share information with us if he's got any. In the meantime, are you still planning to stay in town after all that's happened?"

"Why?" Jack responded. "Are you asking us to leave?"

Parker made a quiet scoffing sound.

The bounty hunters had in fact planned to head back to their homes in Range River tonight and come up with a new plan tomorrow. But the idea of getting pushed out of town got Jack's hackles up.

"What I actually want to ask you is the opposite."

"Oh."

"In an urgent situation like we had tonight—and yesterday—all kinds of surrounding law enforcement agencies will rush to help because that's what we do for each other. But when it comes to long-term investigations or searches, that dynamic changes. The officers' own service areas need them to stay closer to home so they can respond to emergencies in a timely fashion."

"You don't think our department can take care of this?" Parker asked in an even tone.

Silva spared his patrolman a glance before turning back to the bounty hunters. "We've got a good staff here," he began. "But we're a small department. I've only got eight full-time officers and all of them are fairly recent hires. The police force in Blue Mountain has seen a lot of turnover in personnel in the past few years. None of my cops have more than four years' experience in the profession other than Parker here, who moved up from Boise a few months ago. The former police chief, Virgil Agnew, contacted me after the shooting in the park and offered to help out. He's one of a handful of reserve officers we have, so we can make use of him and his skills. Even so, I still think we'll be understaffed for this manhunt."

Jack had been in Blue Mountain on man-

hunts a few times over the years and interacted with some of the officers, but he hadn't
met or worked with the former chief.

"To be blunt, I'm asking you to stay and
help us catch Foster and the other two thugs,"
Silva added.

"What specifically is it that you want us to
do?" Milo asked.

The chief gestured toward Jack and Hayley.
"I'm hoping the four of you will stick with
what you started. Posing as two married couples and talking with people. Keeping things
low-key while you see what you can find out.
It's paid off so far. Knowing Foster was shopping at Bennie Mac's General Store a few
days ago is the only lead we've got. Maybe
something will come of that. Maybe you can
learn something else using that indirect, undercover method."

Hayley shook her head. "I've been thinking
about it and I don't see how we can pull that
off. We've already visited some businesses in
town and told them we were bounty hunters.
Word will get out."

"It might. But if you'll give me a list of
businesses where you talked to people, I'll go
visit them myself and ask that they keep quiet.
Business owners certainly don't want Foster

running loose. I think they'll do what they can to help catch him. Meanwhile, we'll keep the details about the cabin fire and shooting out of the news for as long as we can. We'll keep your names under wraps and report that the cause of the fire is under investigation. We won't mention a possible connection to Foster."

"You can't keep all those facts secret for very long," Parker said.

Silva shrugged. "If these bounty hunters are as good as they seem to believe they are, a few days should be all they need."

Nothing like having a little pressure put on you. But Jack was convinced his team was up for it. He turned to Hayley. "What do you think? Still want to stay married a few more days?"

There was a little smudge of soot on the side of her nose. Her hair was tied back, but strands near her face had come loose and were sticking out in different directions.

She looked exhausted.

And yet, there was nevertheless the steely set of determination in her eyes. She replied with a challenging smile. "I believe I've told you before that I've made up my mind *I'm* going to slap handcuffs on Foster and haul him in. And that means I'll do whatever it takes. So, yes. I'm still in the game."

Jack's heart did a little lurch. She was strong and she was beautiful. And smart. She met his teasing comments with wit of her own, and she didn't back down under pressure.

*Stop.*

Alarm bells went off in Jack's head.

He made a conscious effort to school his features so his growing affection for her didn't show, and to physically lean away from Hayley.

After this case, it would be best if he never worked with her again. He had no room in his life for the sentimental feelings she was stirring up. There was no potential for a future relationship with her.

"So we're included in this plan, too, right?" Katherine asked, indicating herself and her husband.

"Absolutely." Silva nodded. "If you want to take a crack at talking to people in Blue Mountain, too, have at it. Or do whatever research you'd normally do. Just make sure you don't identify yourselves as bounty hunters if you're going to be staying with Jack and Hayley. Because if you do, then that will obviously blow their cover story."

"Right now we don't know where any of us will be staying," Katherine said.

Silva tapped a pen on his desk. "Actually, I can help with that. One of the town's civic organizations organized a modest emergency housing system years ago. It helps people in need and it's a tax break for the hotels, motels and bed-and-breakfasts that donate rooms. One of the participants contacted my office as soon as he heard about the cabin fire.

"George Bitts over at the Bear's Lair Lodge has a family suite available. Two bedrooms, two baths, shared living room. There's a dining hall where you can eat your meals if you want. They have decent security out there so no one's going to sneak up on the place without George or somebody else knowing about it."

"This guy, George, he won't know the truth of who we are and why we're staying in town?" Hayley asked.

"He'll be under the impression that you're simply visitors who have had a traumatic experience and need a place to stay while you regroup."

"I hate the idea of lying to someone who's willing to help out strangers like this," Hayley said.

Silva nodded. "I understand. When this investigation is concluded, the police department will pay them the cost of the suite rental."

"Tell you what," Hayley said, and turned to Jack. "When *I* catch Foster and get paid my recovery fee, I'll use that to cover the cost."

A subdued smile moved across Jack's lips. "*Whoever* catches Foster will use their recovery fee to pay for the suite charges," he said. He turned to Hayley. "Yeah, I'm willing to kick in some money. It will be a small price to pay to keep you alive."

She looked away, but before she did he thought he saw a blush rise in her cheeks.

Part of him hoped that Foster and his companions had fled the area so that Hayley would be safe. But in the long run, having them remain at large would keep her in danger. Realistically, it seemed more likely that Foster was lurking nearby, determined to meet his obsessive goal of killing Hayley before he moved on.

"Good morning...*honey*." Hayley spoke awkwardly as she stepped up to the table in the Bear's Lair Lodge dining room where Jack sat alone sipping a cup of coffee. She hesitated for a moment, aware that other lodge guests and employees might be watching her. She wanted to do a believable job of playing the role of a wife. So, should she kiss him?

Hayley's memories of her parents were wispy. Of course she'd seen plenty of husband and wife interactions on TV, in the movies and in the world around her. But she wasn't exactly up on the nuances on what would make them look like they were a married couple instead of just a man and woman who knew each other.

Tired of overthinking it, she leaned down and gave Jack a light peck on the cheek before she sat down.

He gave her a cheeky smile in return.

"Coffee?" a young woman carrying a pot stopped by and asked.

"Yes, please."

The waitress filled a mug, and Hayley took a sip and savored the bracing effect of the caffeine.

Late last night, or actually very early this morning, George Bitts, owner of the handsomely rugged Bear's Lair Lodge, had welcomed the bounty hunters to his facility believing they were simply two couples visiting town when their rental cabin inexplicably caught fire. He'd ushered them to their third-floor suite, where Hayley and Katherine had shared one bedroom while Jack and Milo had shared the other.

Katherine and Milo had left the lodge a half hour ago heading to Range River with plans to make calls and do research at the office. In particular, they were hoping to get information regarding Barry Foster's visitor and phone call logs for each of the seven times he'd been put in jail since he'd become a legal adult. The idea was to get fresh ideas on who might help him hide in Blue Mountain or elsewhere. They would try to find out the identities of his two accomplices, as well. Maybe one or both had been locked up with him, or come to visit him when he was incarcerated.

Hayley took a look at the menu on the table with the day's breakfast options. "Did you already order?" she asked Jack.

"Yes, *honey*," he said, emphasizing the last word. "Hope you don't mind."

"Not at all, sweetheart," she responded without looking at him, a smile tugging up her lips as they played their little game.

She gave her selection to the waitress, and turned to Jack, ready to talk business. His hand on his mug, he stared intently at the dark brew, obviously absorbed in his thoughts.

The bright sunlight streaming through the nearby window struck his eyes at just the right angle, making them a blue so vibrant they almost looked like they were glowing. The planes and angles of his face looked especially sharp, and intriguing. Hayley's gaze, seemingly out of her control, traveled to his muscled biceps hugged by the sleeves of his dark gray T-shirt.

She tried to ignore the delighted flutter in her chest.

She really needed to get this case wrapped up quickly. Not only so she could put away the bad guys, but so she could get away from the good guy sitting directly in front of her. Jack Colter was starting to appeal to her, but she was not about to follow her heart's promptings. Her brain knew he'd be nothing but trouble.

She *knew* it, and yet, those renegade feelings were there.

Much as she hated to admit it, the man *did* have a touch of charisma.

If she were around him much longer, he'd start to make a mockery of her common sense. And she prided herself on her common sense.

Melanie returned with their food. Thick stacks of buttermilk pancakes with huckleberry syrup and sides of bacon and eggs.

While they were eating, they discussed their plans for the day.

"I saw that you were included in Chief Silva's text this morning saying he'd let us know what he learned after he got a chance to talk to Drew," Hayley said. "What do you want to do in the meantime?"

"We need to generate some leads before Foster comes after you again. First thing I want to do is go back and take a look around the cabin now that it's daylight. Maybe we can find some bit of evidence, a trail leading into the woods, something the cops overlooked."

"All right." Hayley jabbed her fork into her pancakes, but what little bit of appetite she'd had was quickly vanishing. When she'd finally fallen asleep after they'd arrived at the inn, she'd dreamed of fire and smoke. She'd woken up a couple of times with her heart racing and her stomach in knots as the horror of what could have happened grabbed hold of her and wouldn't let go. She'd been through scary situations in the past, but nothing quite like this, when she was the target and her assailant would go to any means to kill her or anyone with her. She forced herself to take a few bites of her breakfast so she would have the energy she needed, and then she set down her fork and switched to just drinking coffee.

"Can we get our bill?" Jack asked the waitress as she passed by when they were ready to leave.

"George told me the lodge is covering the cost of your meals," she told them, continuing on to another table.

A few moments later George Bitts, a tall, slender older gentleman with slightly stooped shoulders and a few wisps of graying hair on his head, came over from the kitchen area and greeted them.

He waved his hands dismissively when Hayley tried to hand him some money and smiled fondly at the two rival bounty hunters whom he believed were a married couple.

Guilt over being less than honest with him threatened to turn Hayley's breakfast to lead in her stomach.

"I'm happy to have you as my guests," George said warmly. It was the same comment he'd made late last night when he'd met the four bounty hunters in the lobby and escorted them up to their suite. "Perhaps one day you'll be in a position to help somebody out," he added. "Doing that would be the best way for you to pay me."

Absolutely, Hayley would do that. But she was also determined to return with the recovery fee she earned after capturing Foster.

Following their brief conversation, George returned to the kitchen and Hayley and Jack headed to the parking lot and climbed into his truck, after Jack left a few bills on the table as a tip.

"Melanie still needs to get paid, even if George won't take our money," he'd said, and shrugged.

Hayley nodded in admiration. She'd have done the same thing, but he beat her to the punch.

The sun looked warm and bright from inside the lodge, but it was chilly outside. A strong breeze blew red and gold leaves from the trees and across the road as they headed back to Peregrine Lake. The die-hard campers might be able to rough it at the lakeside for another three or four weeks, but after that the campground would be closed and winterized in preparation for the arrival of several feet of snow over the months from late fall into early spring.

"Wow, it really looks bad in the light of day, doesn't it," Jack said after they turned the corner and the charred cabin came into view. Yellow-and-black caution tape, along with a notice printed on red paper directing people to stay out of the building, was stretched across the splintered front door.

Seeing the extent of the devastation sent goose bumps rippling across Hayley's skin. "This sounds weird, but it almost seems scarier now than it was when we were in the actual fire," she said softly. "I guess it feels that way because at the time I was so focused on thinking of what to do and how we could escape without getting shot."

"I get it," Jack said. "God had His hand on us. He must have." It was Sunday morning and Jack missed being in church, but he felt compelled to stay on the case and get the dangerous fugitives captured as soon as possible. Hopefully, that would be today.

They got out of the truck and walked around, scanning the ground in front of the cabin and all the way to the edge of the forest at the back of the property. Beyond that, the brush was too thick for them to see much of anything.

They'd been out there for several minutes when Jack reached for Hayley's hand.

She turned to him, feeling disoriented. Because the gesture felt sincere and faked at the same time.

"For the sake of appearances," Jack said. "In case the neighbors are watching."

"Of course," she replied abruptly, feeling irritated for no logical reason. "Why else would I let you hold my hand?"

He grinned in return. Which was also disorienting. Because she couldn't keep herself from smiling back.

They continued searching the area, always on the lookout for Foster or the other assailants who had managed to discover Hayley's whereabouts last night and could probably do it again. Which meant they could be watching them right now.

Other than debris from the fire and trampled-down grass where the emergency vehicles had driven onto the lawn and parked, they saw nothing notable.

"Not even shell casings from the bullets they fired," Jack said. "While they were trying to kill us, they were cool enough to make sure they didn't leave them behind so the police couldn't potentially lift a fingerprint from them. They're getting smarter, less reckless. That doesn't bode well for us."

No one came out of the neighboring cabins to talk with them, which was disappointing.

"This was a bust," Jack said when they finished their search. "We need some new information to help us generate a lead. Maybe Katherine and Milo have uncovered something by now."

He reached for his phone, but before he could place the call a patrol car turned the corner and headed in their direction with Officer Parker at the wheel. Hayley and Jack walked toward the street, and Hayley could see a man in the seat beside Parker. The passenger looked older, a little heavyset, with a neatly trimmed silver beard and gold-wire-framed glasses.

Parker pulled to the side of the road, and rolled down his window. "What are you two doing here?" It wasn't a particularly friendly greeting.

"Just having a look around," Jack said mildly.

"That sign at the front door telling people to stay out applies to bounty hunters as much as anybody else. It is still a crime scene, even though we've kept that aspect under wraps." He eyed them for a moment. "Did you go in there?"

Hayley put her hands on her hips. "Of course not."

The patrol car passenger door opened and the man riding with Parker stepped out.

"Hello, I'm Virgil Agnew, former police chief. And apparently you are the bounty hunters I've heard about." He shook hands with each of them.

"Chief Silva told me he had you two plus a couple of your fellow bounty hunters helping out and I for one am very grateful for that." He cut a glance toward Parker, still seated in the patrol car, and then turned his attention back to Hayley and Jack. "You know a situation is bad when they call the old guy out of mothballs to assist."

Hayley's sour attitude triggered by Parker's rudeness mellowed a little.

"I like to walk a crime scene the day after an incident, too," the former chief said with a glance toward the cabin. "Check for evidence that might have been overlooked. Get a feel for what the bad guys saw, what route they might have taken to arrive, how they may have escaped."

"If you two discovered anything significant you need to report it to the police department," Parker said out his window. "And if you put the citizens of this town in danger because you want to beat us to the capture so you can earn your fugitive recovery fee, I'll make sure you answer for it."

Hayley slid a glance in Jack's direction.

Jack's jaw muscles tensed in response to Parker's comment, but his expression otherwise stayed neutral.

"We understand," Hayley said.

Jack's phone rang. He glanced at the screen and then tapped to answer. "Colter."

He listened with his phone to his ear and Hayley couldn't hear the other side of the conversation. Finally, he thanked the caller, disconnected and turned to Hayley. "That was Chief Silva. He's at Bennie Mac's General Store. He said their security cameras caught a few images of Foster and his two companions. He wants all of us to meet him over there."

"At last," she said as her heart beat faster. "A lead."

Hayley quickly headed toward Jack's truck, more than ready to grab Foster and his thug pals and see that they were locked up. Hopefully, the security images would provide her and the rest of her team with something important.

# SEVEN

"What I want to know is why you didn't report this to the police," Parker said to Drew MacAllen, current proprietor of his family's general store.

Jack cut a glance at the patrolman but made a conscious effort to hide his irritation. Speaking aggressively toward a private citizen who didn't *have* to help the police but was willing to do so made no sense. Beyond that, he was beginning to wonder if the cop had some hidden agenda or just lacked subtlety.

They were in the store's office near a floor-to-ceiling display of scented candles. It smelled like apple cider and pumpkin bread. Hayley and former chief Agnew stood beside Jack, while Parker leaned against the frame of the open doorway. Chief Silva sat at the desk beside Drew with his own small laptop open to a screen with a small spinning icon signaling a slowly downloading file.

"My wife is the newshound in the family," Drew said easily, after sharing a glance with Jack that seemed to indicate he wasn't about to let Parker intimidate him. "She mentioned the shootout and the fire, but I didn't look up any photos. I only pay attention to sports news, weather reports, fishing reports, ski reports, that sort of thing. That way, when people come in to buy their outdoorsy supplies I can give them good information."

"Well, we appreciate your help now," Agnew said soothingly.

Chief Silva made an exasperated sound while staring at his computer. "This thing's taking forever." He turned to Drew. "Why don't you show everybody the images we found on your screen?"

"Sure."

The lanky young man, dressed in a red flannel shirt and sporting black horn-rimmed glasses, looked like a woodsy and techie crossover. While he queued up several segments of security footage to display across two large desktop monitors, Silva explained to the recent arrivals that he and Drew had already matched the security images to Foster's actual sales transaction at the register and determined that he'd paid cash and left no digital financial trail with his purchase.

"What did he buy?" Jack asked.

"Looks like a propane stove and fuel, tents, sleeping bags, freeze-dried food. Heavy coats and boots for himself and his two criminal buddies," Silva said.

"No weapons?"

"A hunting knife," Silva replied. "No guns or ammo. Apparently they were already well supplied with those when they hit town."

"Their purchase had to be a pretty large tab for a cash sale," Parker said. "Didn't that strike you as odd?"

"Not really." Drew kept his attention on his computer screens. "I get a fair number of customers who pay cash. A lot of people do that to help themselves stay within their budget."

"So fugitive Barry Foster came to Blue Mountain with plans to hide out in the wilderness," Jack said, musing out loud. "To stay near Range River where he slipped away from the authorities rather than risk drawing attention to himself on the highway trying to outrun them."

"Or they could have bought that stuff with plans to hit the road," Hayley said. "They'd be prepared to car camp while they made their way out of the region."

"Here we go," Drew said, clicking his mouse to get the security footage rolling and then fast-forwarding to the point when Foster and his criminal friends first showed up.

Everyone who was standing moved closer to the screens to get a better view.

Three generations had built up and added to the shop, so instead of being shaped like a big-box store, it felt more like an old wooden-floored house with several rooms. It was a bit difficult to keep track of the criminals at first, as they disappeared from one video frame and reappeared in another frame with a different angle. The three men wore sunglasses, had their jacket collars flipped up and kept their gazes focused downward as they first entered the store.

"Going that far to avoid being picked up by security cameras kind of defeats the purpose," Hayley commented. "They look like they're there to rob the place."

"No kidding," Drew said with a laugh. "I would have been suspicious, except that it was sunny when they walked in and, as you can see, they pretty quickly took off their shades."

"They realized they were drawing attention to themselves and needed to stop," Jack said quietly while concentrating on the video footage. The three men ambled through a couple of sections of the store, apparently not familiar with the layout. They appeared more focused when they spotted the camping equipment. A salesman went over to speak with them, but they declined his help and he walked away.

"They may not have realized they were being picked up on security video," Drew said. "We keep the cameras subtle. Some store owners figure making them obvious is a theft deterrent. I'm thinking about going that route but I like customers feeling comfortable, not watched."

Jack listened to Drew while continuing to focus on the videos, his attention riveted on the two accomplices who'd apparently been with Foster since before the initial ambush in the forest. So far, neither the cops nor the bounty hunters had any lead on them and that fact had been driving Jack crazy. He wanted the two men traveling with Foster identified. If they weren't bail jumpers, then, as Parker would no doubt be quick to point out, Jack and his crew would not be authorized to apprehend either of them. But knowing who they were might lead the bounty hunters to people who were assisting or even hiding the fugitives.

"There," Silva called out. "Right there the shorter one turns his face upward."

Drew froze the image so they could take a lingering look.

The guy had blond hair and a darker mustache and brown eyes. Jack had never seen him before. "He look familiar to anybody?"

No one recognized him.

At Jack's request, Drew emailed him the clearest image they could find of Mustache Man. They went through the same process again a few minutes later when the other thug, slightly taller, with black hair and a thin beard glanced toward a camera.

"Oh, good," Silva said after a moment. "My copy of your security files have finally finished downloading."

"Where's your outside security footage?" Parker asked. "Maybe we can see them arriving or leaving. Get a shot of their vehicle."

"We've got a fixed camera on each of our doors," Drew said, bringing up the images. "But nothing aimed at the parking lot or the surrounding streets."

"Some of the interior shots catch part of the view through your glass doors," Hayley said. "How about we look at footage before and after the creeps come into your store, this time watching for passing vehicles. It's a long shot, but it's something."

The images weren't very clear, but a few minutes later they had a short list of the color of vehicles they'd glimpsed along with their best guesses on makes and models.

"Does the town have any traffic cams?" Hayley asked.

"No," Parker answered tightly.

Chief Silva turned to look at her. "It's been in my budget request and will be until we finally get some."

Agnew shook his head. "A traffic camera system like that can be awfully expensive."

"You'll let us know if the facial recognition database gives you the names of either of these guys, right?" Jack asked Silva.

"Of course." Silva closed up his laptop case. "And if any of your informants recognize the men in those pictures, you be sure and let us know."

"We will," Jack said. He and Hayley voiced their appreciation to Drew before leaving the store and getting into Jack's truck.

"Let me get these images of the two extra thugs sent to Katherine and Milo." Jack sat behind the steering wheel, focused on his phone screen. "Then I'll send them to you, too, so you can forward them to whoever you need to."

"I'll forward them to my brothers and Wade, as well," Hayley said. "And Jonah and Lorraine at the Range River Bail Bonds office. Maybe they'll recognize one or both of them. It's worth a try."

Jack agreed. Right now *everything* seemed worth a try.

If Foster and his companions had tried to make a quick getaway after the fire and shooting last night, Jack was pretty sure one of the law enforcement agencies in the region would have seen them by now. Blue Mountain was relatively isolated. Granted, there was the railroad line near the edge of town and that was one means of escape. But modern freight trains were not all that easy to jump onto, and their schedules were unpredictable.

There was only one county highway that passed through town and continued onward. The rest of the roads either eventually looped back into town, dead-ended at the edge of town or turned into dirt roads that weren't so easy to navigate unless you had the right kind of vehicle.

Chances were good that the bad guys were hanging around, watching and waiting. With Foster intent on getting to Hayley.

"Maribel suggested I remind you to be careful," Katherine said to Hayley with a slight smile. "I'm not sure if she meant be careful about the fugitive we're chasing or be careful about your marriage to Jack Colter."

"What?" Hayley said, the word sounding like a squeak.

The two women were outside the Bear's Lair Lodge, grabbing suitcases out of the rear compartment of the SUV that Katherine and Milo had driven back from Range River. Rain clouds were gathering overhead, throwing the area around the lodge and the nearby craft and curio shops into a deep blue dusky light. The guys were on the enclosed deck on the other side of the lodge, on a video call with a couple of other bail bondsmen in the region, showing them the images of Foster's still-unidentified two accomplices to see if anybody had any ideas about them.

Since the bounty hunters' stay in Blue Mountain had been extended, Hayley had asked Maribel Fast Horse to pack some additional clothes for her. Katherine and Milo had dropped by to grab them and bring them along on their return drive to the lodge. At the rate things were going—specifically their *lack* of leads—it looked like Hayley and Jack might be wandering around the small town trying to talk to people and glean information for a while.

"Why would I have to be careful about a fake marriage?" Hayley demanded as she grabbed the handles of a small satchel-style suitcase and a toiletries case from the back of the SUV. "I've worked undercover before. Maribel knows I can pull it off."

"*Somebody* might have mentioned to her that the two of you seem to be getting along awfully well." Katherine's smile grew wider.

At a loss for words, Hayley just huffed out a breath.

The words were on the tip of her tongue to tell Katherine just how unattractive she found Jack Colter. Well, okay, physically he was kind of attractive. But he was full of himself. And obnoxious. The man carried out his job in ways that added to the shady reputation bounty hunters held in some people's minds.

But the defensive words didn't quite make their way out of her mouth.

Because, really, was he *that* obnoxious or was he just a man who liked teasing people? He seemed to enjoy teasing her, particularly. But she had to admit the guy didn't just dish it out. He could take it, too, when she teased him back.

And though she'd been watching for any sign of him stepping beyond the bounds of professionalism as he carried out his job, she hadn't actually witnessed him doing that.

Well, not yet.

Oh, man. Was she going soft while she was on this assignment?

Was she starting to think she actually *liked* the guy who was her family's arch business rival?

She saw marriage on her horizon, but it still felt a long way off. She wanted to prove herself to her brother Connor after all he'd done for her in his own life. She wanted to be the best bounty hunter in the region.

"When did you and Maribel get so chummy?" Hayley asked, feeling like she needed to grab hold of this conversation and redirect it. "I don't remember her ever mentioning that she knew you."

A couple of cars drove by in the lodge's parking lot. It was evening, so they were probably guests looking to check in for the night.

"Milo and I stopped by the hospital to check on Luther. Maribel was there visiting him. He was awake and able to talk a little. I heard her telling Jessica that the entire Range River Bail Bonds family would be praying for his recovery and they would be more than happy to help Jessica or anyone else in the family if they needed anything. So, later in the day, when we stopped by the inn to grab your extra clothes and such, she already felt like a friend. She's just so easy to open up to."

Yeah, Maribel had that effect on people.

"And, well, I might have mentioned that you and Jack seemed to be growing a wee bit fond of one another."

Hayley's eyes narrowed, but before she could utter her words of protest someone wrapped an arm around her from behind. What was going on? Was this a joke?

It was deadly serious. The man was pulling her against him so that her arms were pinned to her sides as he slapped a hand over her mouth.

In front of her, a man who'd been crouched down and hiding behind a car shot out and lunged at Katherine. It was Foster's accomplice. The blond one with the mustache.

Katherine grabbed her gun clear of her holster, but Hayley saw her training kick in as the Eagle Rapids bounty hunter took the extra few seconds to make certain no innocent by-stander was in her line of fire. That slight hesitation was all it took for Mustache Man to knock her to the ground. Hard.

Hayley bit the hand across her mouth while she twisted and stomped on her assailant's foot.

The attacker moved his hand only to fist it and punch her in the jaw. The short distance of the throw and the odd angle meant that the blow didn't do a lot of damage, but the impact was enough to make Hayley's head spin. She screamed for help, not at all certain if any-one was within hearing distance to come to their aid.

There was a rumble of thunder and then rain came down, not in gentle drops but as a curtain of water. It was enough to clear Hay-ley's head a little, and she tried twisting again and reaching for her gun.

Too late. The assailant grabbed it first, along with the small canister of pepper spray she'd had clipped to the belt loop on her jeans.

Then the guy kicked the back of her knee, forcing her leg to buckle, and she fell to the ground. Rolling to her side, she could see her attacker. It was Barry Foster.

The thug looked much worse than he had just a couple of days ago, with dark circles under his eyes. His clothes were rumpled and stained and the reddish bristles on his head and chin had grown out further and were looking spiky and dirty.

He'd probably been hiding in the woods. Obsessed enough to stay in town and try to kill her rather than make his escape.

And right now he stood over her with her own gun pointed at her. He flicked the safety off and rested his finger on the trigger. "You aren't as smart as you think."

Hayley used her hands to push herself up to a sitting position, sliding one hand close to her right hip. Her phone was in her back pocket. It was the closest thing within her grasp she could use as a weapon. Maybe it was a stupid idea, but quitting was not an option.

There was a moment when she could almost hear her brother Connor's voice. *Ryans don't quit.*

She grabbed the phone and flung it. Foster's apparent fatigue worked to her advantage. He was slow in reacting, and it landed at his right eye.

*Bang!*

He took a staggering step and pulled the

trigger right as the phone smacked him. His shot went wide.

He took another step to steady himself and aimed again.

*Dear Lord*, Hayley whispered the plea, excruciatingly aware at this moment of how little control anyone actually had over their life.

Katherine managed to temporarily blind Mustache Man with a shot of pepper spray. In an instant, she moved behind Foster, grabbing him in a choke hold and reaching for his gun.

The bail jumper flailed his arm and pulled the trigger two more times, the shots narrowly missing Hayley.

"Run!" Katherine yelled, still grappling with him.

There were sounds of doors opening at the lodge, of people coming out into the parking lot.

Hayley hesitated. She didn't want to abandon her friend. But there was no way she could move toward Katherine without almost certainly getting shot. And she definitely couldn't stay in place without getting shot, either.

Katherine couldn't hold him forever. She wasn't strong enough, and then what? He'd try to kill her and the other bounty hunters.

Hayley regretted not acting sooner to distance herself from her colleagues. Foster wanted her. Staying near her fellow bounty hunters just put them in jeopardy.

"Go! *Now!*" Katherine hollered.

Hayley scrambled to get her footing beneath her and then she jumped up and ran, moving in a zigzag pattern as she heard more shots fired in her direction. Good. He was after her and just her. The wide expanse of the lodge parking lot seemed too risky to run across. Heading in that direction could get civilians shot. Beyond that, she didn't know the position of Foster's accomplice. She hadn't seen him yet, but he could be right there in the parking lot, watching and waiting for his chance to take a shot at her.

She headed for the closest edge of the lodge property, where there were a few trees, and beyond them a narrow lane that used to be the main carriage road from downtown to the old sawmill. The short section of road with its Old West–themed stores and hand-craft shops would be closed up for the evening by now.

Pumping her legs as hard as she could, she did her best to focus on her goal of finding a place to take cover while fighting the residual dizziness from being punched by Foster.

She was nearly to a building where she could stop, hunker down and catch her breath.

Maybe all the bad guys had already been captured by now. She hoped that was the case.

She slowed her pace a little, already regretting her decision to obey Katherine's command and run. She should have stayed to help her follow bounty hunter fight. Although at that particular moment, there hadn't appeared to be any reasonable option other than getting out of the range of Foster's gunfire.

The pounding in her ears eased. She could hear sounds behind her in the direction of the lodge, but they were indistinct. Voices, it sounded like. People yelling to one another. The sound of vehicles moving into the parking lot.

Perhaps the police had arrived. She knew from experience that they oftentimes rolled up to an active shooter scene without flashing lights or sirens.

She stopped and turned to look, and her breath caught in her chest.

Barry Foster jogged toward her at an easy pace, and when his gaze connected with hers, she felt his murderous intent like a jolt to her stomach.

She turned and darted toward the nearest

building, a red barnlike structure with signs advertising that it was a glassblower's shop.

It was locked up and empty.

So were most of the other businesses, although there were a few cars on the street and in the small parking lot. There were lights on in second-story windows in a couple of the buildings, but there was no one in sight.

She bolted across the street, and into a shadowy passage between a toy store and a tea shop.

Foster was gaining on her. She could hear his footfalls slapping against the pavement and then splashing as he hit the puddles already forming in the sudden downpouring of rain.

"I'll find you!" Foster yelled, the sound of his voice channeled and amplified as he ran into the passage behind her. "How do you like being the one hunted, *bounty hunter*?"

Desperation kicked in and Hayley considered screaming for help, but that would only make it easier for him to pinpoint her location.

He was taller than her, with longer legs and a longer stride. He could run faster and he *would* catch up with her.

She could smash a window, and break into

a building, but then she would be trapped. Foster would find her and kill her before help arrived.

Still running, she turned into the narrow alley, raced past the back sides of a couple of buildings and then turned again, hoping he hadn't seen her in the darkness and rain.

She was back on the street front side of the businesses again. To her left was a Victorian-style house with a wraparound porch. And on that porch were wooden birdhouses. Big ones, multistoried, obviously crafted here and offered for sale.

That's where she would hide.

Hayley raced up the walkway to the heavy chain holding a closed sign and hopped over it to get to the porch. She ducked down between a couple of the biggest birdhouses, which were a good three feet in height, curling into a ball as tightly as she could, hoping that Foster would run by without spotting her.

He didn't.

# EIGHT

Foster must have seen Hayley run up onto the porch. He took the exact same path she did and headed right toward her. She sprang to her feet and looked for a gun in his hand, ready to charge him and wrest it from him as a last resort.

She didn't see one. Instead, she saw the glinting blade of a knife.

Maybe he'd dropped the gun. Or run out of bullets. Maybe he wanted to kill her quietly so he didn't give away his location.

Whatever the reason, she was nevertheless backed into a corner on the porch with nowhere to run.

He stalked toward her, raising the knife.

With nothing else to use as a weapon, she grabbed one of the tall birdhouses by its base and swung it at him, aiming for the knife in his hand, hoping to knock it out of his grasp.

He jumped back and cursed.

She swung again, this time aiming for his face.

He ducked out of the way, but then he turned toward the street. At that moment, Hayley realized she heard sirens.

Foster turned back to her, an expression of fury twisting his features. He lunged at her one more time with the knife, and she blocked the attempt again with the birdhouse, gritting her teeth and putting all of her strength into swinging it.

Cursing again, Foster turned and sprinted for the barrier chain, leaped over it and ran down the street.

Hayley dropped the birdhouse. Exhausted and relieved, she was tempted to collapse into a sitting position on the porch and wait for the cops to arrive.

*He'll get away.*

She couldn't let that happen.

She climbed over the chain barrier and took off running after her fugitive. With no weapon and no phone, she had no idea what she'd do when she caught him. But she couldn't just let him vanish, only to attempt to kill her—or someone else—again.

Rain poured down hard, and in the dusky

light it was difficult to see Foster. He had a good head start on her.

The sirens were getting closer. As she ran, she thought she heard someone yelling. Then she realized it was Jack, calling out her name. It sounded like he was roughly parallel to her, in the alleyway behind the shops, in the direction of the lodge.

*"Here!"* was all she could manage to holler out, needing all the oxygen she could draw in to keep running.

Seconds later, he called her name again. She couldn't spare the extra breath to answer. Foster was close to disappearing in front of her, and if she didn't draw upon her final reserves of strength to sprint and capture him, he'd vanish.

*Faster!* She pushed herself to run harder, but her pace didn't change to any discernible degree. She was just too tired.

Ahead, Foster reached an intersecting road.

A motorcycle darted out in front of him. It slid to a stop in a potholed section of street, tossing up a wave of watery mud that blew back toward the rider. He flipped his helmet's visor, which must have gotten doused with the sludge.

Foster stopped before the motorcycle could hit him, moved around it and continued running.

The motorcyclist lurched forward at an awkward angle and got in front of him again. It was impossible to tell if he was getting in Foster's way on accident or on purpose.

The intervention was enough for Hayley to nearly catch up with Foster as he again maneuvered around the motorcyclist and resumed running.

The sirens were getting louder. The police were almost here. *Thank You, Lord!*

Ahead, Foster sped up and a figure darted out of the alley, tackling him and knocking him to the ground. The thug struggled to get up, but Jack punched him, knocking him back down. Milo darted out from that same alley a few moments later.

Hayley's footsteps fumbled because she was so exhausted, and her lungs burned as she fought to catch her breath. Her body was forcing her to slow down.

She glanced in the direction of the motorcyclist who'd intervened with Foster, and slowed even more to get a better look at him.

He turned in her direction and she saw his face. Her job required a good memory for faces and this one looked familiar.

She slowed even more and started to walk

toward him. And then she stopped in her tracks. She was looking at a wanted man.

He was a dangerous fugitive who'd jumped bail and vanished fifteen years ago. His old booking photo was on the wall at Range River Bail Bonds along with the photos of several other criminals the bounty hunters hoped to apprehend someday.

Did this man actually have a connection to Barry Foster, or was the intersecting of their paths at this exact moment just a bizarre co-incidence?

"Kris Ridge!" Hayley called out the wanted man's name before she could stop herself, thinking she would somehow place him under arrest. His appearance at this time in this situation was mind-boggling, but she would take action now and try to comprehend what had happened later.

He pulled a gun and pointed. He took a quick glance toward the cops that had arrived at the end of the street where Jack had tackled Foster. Then he flipped down the visor on his helmet, swiped a gloved hand across it to wipe away the grime, gunned the motorcycle and sharply turned it around before speeding away.

Hayley's jaw dropped. *What just happened?* The events didn't seem real.

But they *were* real.

She resumed walking and caught up with Jack, Milo and the handcuffed and subdued former fugitive Barry Foster.

"Looks like another capture for Eagle Rapids bounty hunters," Jack said with a broad smile. "Plus we got his two accomplices over by the lodge. Looks like this pursuit is wrapped up."

Hayley just stared at him, the image of Kris Ridge still in her mind. She was already starting to doubt herself and what she thought she'd seen. It didn't seem possible.

"I'm kidding," Jack said after a moment. "You're the reason we have him in custody. You deserve the credit."

"You go ahead and take credit for capturing this guy," Hayley said, gesturing toward Foster who was glaring at her. "He's no big deal." The last thing she wanted to do was feed this murderous criminal's ego.

It was horrifying to know that the evil-minded person in front of her had murdered two human beings. Then, after he went on the run, he'd intentionally put Luther Garcia in the hospital. Had very nearly killed him.

And then he'd almost ended the lives of Hayley and her fellow bounty hunters by setting the cabin on fire and shooting at them.

What huge, horrible actions. And yet, what a small, pitiful character he was.

Once fugitives were captured, even the scariest ones typically shrank down until they seemed less like terrifying monsters and more like selfish jerks throwing dangerous, childish tantrums.

That was certainly the case with this loser.

Foster's expression had become even angrier after Hayley's comment describing him as not a big deal. In return, she made a point of smiling at him. Just to remind the murderer that this time the good guys won.

Once her adrenaline levels lowered, relief over the fact that he was no longer at large would settle in and she'd feel a sense of accomplishment.

Right now her mind was on other things. Chief among them was her concern for Katherine. If Milo was here, his wife must be okay. Still, Hayley wanted to confirm that for herself.

The police arrived and took custody of Foster.

One of the cops offered the bounty hunters

a ride back to the lodge so they could change into dry clothes before going to the police station to give their statements. Milo took him up on offer, but Hayley had things to think about. She let them know she wanted to walk. It wasn't that far to the lodge, she was already soaked, anyway, and the rain was falling more gently now. It would be a good way to unwind.

"I'll go with you," Jack said, and before she could protest, he matched his stride to hers as they set off.

"You all right?" he asked after they'd covered a short distance.

"Kris Ridge," she said after a moment.

"Kris Ridge?" He gave her a confused look. "The fugitive every bounty hunter in this region of the county has been wanting to capture for the last fifteen years? What about him?"

"I just saw him. He was the man on the motorcycle back there. You must have seen him. He kept getting in Foster's way. I don't know if that was on purpose or not."

Jack didn't respond at first. And then he asked, "Did you recognize him because of his eyes?"

She nodded. Ridge's eyes were very distinctive. "He pulled a gun on me, but then looked toward the cops and after that he turned around and sped away."

Jack was giving her an odd look. "You didn't want to say anything about it to the cops?" he asked.

"They wouldn't believe me." She shook her head. "I almost don't believe me. But I'm not mistaken." She turned to him. "Why would Kris Ridge be here? He got away with a fortune. Everybody's been assuming for years that he got out of the country and has been living the high life in some exotic location."

"Ridge is a highly intelligent, merciless killer," Jack said. "Please tell me he didn't get a good look at your face."

"He did. And I said his name. He knows I recognized him."

"He's going to want to shut you up before you can convince anybody else that you saw him."

Hayley sighed heavily. The bounty hunters had assumed Foster and his two companions were their only threat and biggest worry in Blue Mountain. Apparently they'd been wrong.

"Kris Ridge? I know I've heard that name. But I don't know any details about him." The person speaking was a patrol officer with the name tag Walker pinned on her uniform. Jack thought she looked young—clearly a rookie—and she'd been one of the responding officers to arrest Foster.

She'd piped up in the awkward silence after Hayley told Chief Silva about seeing Ridge.

Jack and Hayley were in the police chief's office along with Milo and Katherine. Officer Walker was also there, along with Officer Parker and former chief Agnew. On the drive over to the police station, Hayley told Jack that she was going to tell Silva about seeing Ridge. Milo and Katherine, sitting in the back seat, had been absolutely flabbergasted by the news.

Right now, everyone else who'd just heard Hayley repeat her story—and actually knew who Kris Ridge was—seemed stunned.

"You know what? I'll just do a little research about Ridge online," Walker finally said. "I'll inform myself."

"Kris Ridge worked for an armored car company," Hayley explained. "He and the two partners he usually worked with were told a couple of days ahead of time that they'd be transporting a large collection of gold coins. The heir to one of the nearby silver mines was getting older and had decided to cash them out and have some fun with the money. He had a buyer in Seattle. The armored car company was supposed to transport the coins to the Spokane, Washington, airport. At that point they were supposed to be put on a private plane and securely transported over to the coast."

"Let me guess," Walker said. "This Ridge guy killed his partners and stole the coins."

"Yes, and he was smart about it," Jack interjected. The crime had occurred when Jack was starting out as a bounty hunter and he'd wanted to capture Ridge so badly that he'd studied every detail he could find about the man and his horrible crime. "He shot his partners, removed the coins from the armored car and hid them, then staged the scene to match the description he gave the cops about how they were robbed by some mysterious gang of thieves. He even shot himself in the leg to give his story some added credibility."

"And the cops fell for it?" Walker asked, an expression of disbelief on her face.

"Some did, but some didn't. Security footage made Ridge look suspicious. So he changed his story, claimed he'd actually been blackmailed into cooperating with the mysterious robbers. He said that he and his family were threatened. It didn't fly. He was arrested for aiding and abetting an armed robbery. He got out on bail and actually stayed in town, probably thought he could beat the rap. Until the cops uncovered enough evidence to prove he'd acted alone and killed his coworkers. Before they could arrest him again, and charge him with the murders, he vanished."

"And no one ever saw him again until tonight?" Walker asked.

Jack nodded.

"Why didn't you mention seeing him when the officers were there arresting Foster?" Chief Silva spoke his words slowly and he watched Hayley closely, as though he didn't quite trust her or what she was saying.

"It's kind of hard to believe, don't you think?" Hayley said. "I'm having trouble believing it and *I* saw him."

"Ridge's last known photo is fifteen years old," Parker said. "How could you possibly get a glimpse of him, when it's dark and raining and you've just been running for your life, and recognize him?"

"His picture's on the wall at our office. I've been looking at it for a long time. I've studied his features."

"Because you wanted to earn the million-dollar bounty?" Parker asked cynically.

"I would not mind that kind of payout." Hayley spared him a glance, and then turned back to Silva. "But I want to capture the man because he killed two men. Left behind two widows and five children without their husbands and fathers. And yes, I recognized him even though it was dark and rainy. Something triggered in my memory the second I saw the motorcycle rider's heterochromia."

"Hetero...what?" Officer Walker asked.

"Kris Ridge's eyes are two different colors," Hayley said. "One is light brown, the other is medium green. Heterochromia is not common," she continued. "To have that same color combination, along with Ridge's facial features? It's not somebody else, it's him."

"Let's table this whole issue of whether or not you saw Kris Ridge for the moment," Silva said. "Right now I want to interrogate Foster and the thugs who've been working with him."

"Have you got identification on the two accomplices?" Jack asked.

Silva nodded. "Peter Hofer and Lee Weser. Both have done time on drug distribution charges." He picked up a tablet and nodded at Parker. "Let's get going. They're going to be transported down to county jail in Range

River shortly, but I want a crack at talking to them before they go. Obviously, I'd like to get confessions out of all three of them. Beyond that, since Foster seems to be the ringleader of the crew, I want to know if there was a specific reason he came to Blue Mountain. And if anyone here has been helping him."

Silva and Parker headed down the hall to the interrogation room. The others followed but then stopped short and packed into the small room next door where they could listen in and watch the questioning through a one-way mirror.

Agnew, who stood beside Jack, glanced at Hayley and shook his head. "If that really was Ridge that she saw, I have to believe that he just recently got to town. Maybe to meet with Foster for some reason." He took off his glasses, rubbed his eyes and then put them back on. "I don't want to find out that he was here for the past fifteen years, right under my nose while I was chief of police, and I didn't see him. That nobody in my department saw him. Especially with the different-colored eyes. I'd forgotten about that. It's definitely something that stands out."

"He could wear colored contacts sometimes to hide that," Jack offered.

On the other side of the glass, it was quickly clear that Foster had no intention of talking with Silva. He refused to answer questions and demanded a lawyer. The accomplices, Hofer and Weser, did the same.

While the thugs were brought in and then out of the interrogation room so they could be questioned individually, Jack's thoughts kept returning to Agnew's comments. Had Kris Ridge come to Blue Mountain to meet with Barry Foster and his criminal friends? Was there some kind of larger conspiracy going on here?

And how could all of that affect Hayley's safety?

"So you'll be handing Foster and the other two over to the Range River County Sheriff's Department?" Jack asked Chief Silva after his attempts to question the three criminals was over.

"Yes," Silva said. "Transport van will be here at 7:00 a.m. Foster was the only bail jumper out of the three. And I'm assuming you'll need documentation from me so you can collect your recovery fee from the company that issued their bond."

Jack wanted to make it clear he wasn't

just asking for himself. He glanced over and made eye contact with Hayley before nodding. "That's right, *we* will."

Agnew had already gone home for the night. Silva turned to Parker, who was lingering nearby. "In the three years I've been here, I don't remember dealing with a bounty hunter who'd actually captured somebody. Do you know how to access the form for that?"

"No, sir," Parker replied. "You've been here longer than I have, so I haven't seen a bounty turned in, either."

"Where did you come here from?" Jack asked Parker.

"I moved up here from Boise."

"What brought you to Blue Mountain?" Jack felt the inkling of an idea in the back of his mind, but it wasn't clear yet. He just found himself thinking about Parker's aversion to the bounty hunters.

"I thought I'd enjoy small-town policing on the edge of the wilderness," Parker said. "And it turns out I do."

The two lawmen, along with the four bounty hunters, headed back to Silva's office.

"We can get the forms we need from the administrative people at the county jail after they take custody of the prisoners," Jack said as they walked, picking up the thread of that topic of conversation. "They're used to working with us." He turned to Hayley. "But they'll be shocked when we claim equal credit for Range River Bail Bonds and Eagle Rapids Bail Bonds making the recovery."

"So you really are going to acknowledge my small part in chasing down the fugitive." Hayley lifted a reddish-blond eyebrow. "How generous."

When it came time to file the official paperwork, Jack intended to acknowledge that the capture and the recovery fee were entirely hers. He realized he was just the guy who got to tackle Foster and put on the cuffs.

When they reached Silva's office, the chief dropped into the chair behind his desk and then took in the four bounty hunters with a sweeping glance. "It's late. Why are you all still here?"

"Kris Ridge," Hayley said. "I want to get back to that. Are you going to alert the FBI? Will you have your officers actively look for him? Do you intend to let the surrounding police agencies know he's in the region?"

"No. To all three of those questions." Silva rubbed his hand over his face.

Hayley, who was perched on the edge of a

visitor chair across from him, pulled herself up until she was sitting ramrod straight. "You don't believe I actually saw him."

"No, I do not." The chief glanced at Parker, and then took a deep breath. "Look, you've been through a lot over the last few days. Not to mention the fact that your life was in danger at the moment you saw the motorcyclist. Even though Foster was running away from you, he could have turned and attacked you at any moment. Plus it was dark and raining at the time. And I don't buy your claim that you're sure you saw him. Nobody has a current picture of Ridge. And thinking you saw the two different eye colors, that could have been a trick of the light or a reflection or something."

"Even if you don't believe me, why can't you have your officers be on the lookout for him, anyway?" Hayley asked. "Why can't you alert the other law enforcement agencies of a possible sighting? What could it hurt?"

"It could hurt the people of this little town," Silva said. "*My* town." He set his hands on his desk. "We're growing. People are moving here from all over the place, and while that definitely brings some good with it, it also brings some problems. All kinds of crimes, from commercial burglary to drug dealing, are up. Those are real. Kris Ridge is a phantom. I'm not sending officers on what could be a wild-goose chase, and getting other agencies involved would mean using my resources to help them."

"The man on the motorcycle pointed a gun at me," Hayley said. "That should be reason enough to go after him."

Jack shuddered at the thought. It was upsetting enough to know that someone pointed a gun at Hayley and threatened her life. The fact that the threatening thug was a murderous fugitive with every reason to kill her before she could convince anyone that he was alive and here in this town made it even worse.

"Noted," Silva said wearily. "A man who looks like you imagine Kris Ridge would look like right now pointed a gun at you. Can you give me a description of the motorcycle?"

"It was a street bike. Black. Yamaha. I didn't notice any modifications."

"Did you get the license plate number on it?"

"No."

"I'm afraid there's not a whole lot I can do with that." Silva sat back in his chair, his features softening slightly. "Look, I appreciate everything you and your partners did to help capture Foster and his thug friends. But I have to manage my resources carefully. What you've told me just isn't enough to start a manhunt for Kris Ridge."

"But you don't mind if I hang around town and look for him myself?" Hayley said. It sounded more like a statement than a question.

"If you find something you can substantiate, let me know. Otherwise, as long as you work within the limits of the law, go ahead and do your bounty hunter thing. Search for Kris Ridge if you want to."

Hayley got to her feet. Jack, Milo and Katherine had been standing the whole time. After a round of goodbyes, they left the chief's office and headed for the main exit.

"It doesn't matter to me what anybody thinks," Hayley said tightly as the trio stepped outside. "I am going to capture Kris Ridge."

"Oh, I doubt that," Jack said, as they made their way down the steps.

She turned and shot him a glare.

He winked in return. "I'm going to capture him before you do."

"You believe I saw him." A broad smile

crossed her lips so full of relief and appreciation that Jack felt his heart swell in his chest.

The warmth of emotion was almost enough to cover the cold fear that she would be in grave danger the whole time.

Almost, but not enough.

Jack was definitely worried.

# NINE

"Why don't you tell me what's really going on?" George stood in the living room of the suite at the Bear's Lair Lodge with his arms crossed over his chest and his eyebrows raised.

The bounty hunters had returned to the lodge from the police station near midnight with their future intentions still open for discussion. Katherine and Milo were on board with the goal of capturing Kris Ridge, but they hadn't all agreed on a specific plan yet.

Hayley figured a couple of things were certain. One was that her pretend marriage to Jack Colter was over. Which gave her a weird feeling of loneliness combined with relief. And maybe disappointment. Her other certainty was that the bounty hunters would no longer be welcome at the lodge since last night's events and the subsequent interactions with the police must have made it plain to George that these guests weren't who they'd pretended to be.

So his demand for an explanation right now was no surprise.

"I'm sorry we lied to you." Hayley was the first to reply. Maybe because she'd felt bad about misleading the man even if it was for a good reason. "I'm sure the police told you our story."

George shook his head. "The officers who showed up to arrest those two men in the parking lot involved in the attack on you two ladies—" his glance quickly swept over to Katherine and then back to Hayley "—didn't tell me much. I know there was a big ruckus in town—I heard the sirens. I know Chief Silva is busy right now but he'll answer my questions when he has time. Instead of making me wait, how about you explain everything to me right now?"

Hayley turned to Jack. "What do you think?" She wasn't asking him to give her permission. She was giving him a chance to offer his input, a courtesy she'd extend to any partner she was working with.

"We might as well tell him."

Hayley gave a quick, general summary of the events since they'd first hit town.

When she was finished, George uncrossed his arms and took a deep breath.

"Okay."

"Okay, *what*?" Hayley asked after a moment of silence.

He shrugged. "I can get over the fact that you've lied to me from the beginning. I provide housing for people in trouble. I'm told all kinds of stories that I know aren't true. Sometimes someone needs a fake identity to hide from stalkers or anybody else intending them harm. Now that I understand the situation, and it doesn't seem likely that my other guests will be put in danger, I can continue to go along with your undercover operation. So, are you going to need this suite any longer?"

The four bounty hunters exchanged looks.

"We may have further business in the area," Hayley said cautiously. There was no way she was going to tell him about her sighting of Kris Ridge.

"But the reason for us staying in the lodge is that it makes it easier for Jack and me to keep up the appearance of being a married couple considering a permanent move to town. It's a nonthreatening cover that we hope will make people more likely to talk openly with us. But it looks like that option is no longer open."

"Why not?"

"Our covers have probably been blown with the arrest of Barry Foster," Katherine said, picking up a sweater from the back of a chair where it had been laying and putting it on. "I imagine our names and faces have made the local news. Everybody has a phone, everybody takes pictures. Not much we can do about it."

"You might not *need* to do anything about it," George said thoughtfully. "As soon as the attack happened in the parking lot and one of the guests called the cops and the arrests were made, I hopped on the internet to see what I could learn." He grinned self-consciously. "I typed my search terms even faster when I heard the sirens converging over on Carriage Street. Eventually the Police Blotter section of the town's online newspaper had a short entry about the arrest of the two guys here in the lodge parking lot and also the arrest of the bail jumper who was wanted out of Range River. But I didn't see anything about any of you."

"Well, now," Milo said from his spot on

the sofa. "That might change things." He was already scrolling his phone. "Yeah, information about the arrests is here, but they only mention the cops. They've left our names out of it."

Hayley glanced in Jack's direction. He lifted his brows inquiringly, but there wasn't much more she wanted to say in front of George.

"If you'd like to continue to stay here, I wouldn't have a problem with that," George drawled. "Of course you'd have to pay the bounty hunter's room rate, which is a little higher than the standard rate." He grinned. "I figure that's a business expense for you and from my end of things it'll help me assist people in the future who are *genuinely* desperate for a place to stay."

"We'll need to discuss it," Hayley said.

"Take your time." George walked to the door. "I'm billing you for tonight, so you've got until morning to ponder things."

"This lodge is as secure a place to stay as we're going to find in town," Jack said as soon as George shut the door behind him.

He looked at Hayley, concern on his face. She knew he was worried about Ridge having seen her, and potentially targeting her.

And while she appreciated the concern, she also bristled a little at it. She was capable. She was careful.

And she was especially grateful that he'd believed her.

Milo and Katherine had politely made their skepticism known on the drive back to the lodge, but they were ultimately willing to join the chase.

"I agree that this is a good place to stay," Hayley said to Jack. "I don't see any reason to move to another location in Blue Mountain. If we chose to return to our homes in Range River every night and then come back the next morning instead, the drive back and forth would eat up a lot of our time. So, yeah, I'd like for us to stay."

"It's hard to believe that we—or rather you—would just stumble across one of the most wanted fugitives in this part of the county," Milo said, shaking his head. "Even harder to believe he would be right here under our noses."

Hayley agreed. It *was* hard to believe. Capturing him was a one in a million long shot that she didn't want to miss.

Right now she had no idea how to go looking for him. But maybe she didn't have to.

Maybe just by being in town, and making herself visible, she would lure out Ridge.

He couldn't have survived this long on the run with his head in the sand. He must know who she was. Or he would have a way of figuring it out. She'd seen him and recognized him. That made her a threat. But it would take time for her to convince more people that she'd seen him. He would know that. He would come looking for her so he could silence her, possibly by way of something that looked like a random event, so that the question of whether or not he had ever truly been sighted in Blue Mountain would remain a mystery.

"It's settled, then," Jack said. "We'll stay here. At least for another day or two." He looked at Hayley and smiled broadly. "Good news, honey, the marriage is back on."

Oh, yes, the pretend marriage. One more tricky element Hayley needed to manage in a life that was getting more complicated by the minute.

"The age progression software we've got back at the office should get us some helpful images of Ridge to show people when we need to," Jack said to Hayley the next morning shortly after they were seated for breakfast in the lodge's dining room. "Plan for an online meeting sometime today so you can suggest whatever tweaks need to be made so the images look like Ridge as you saw him last night."

Admittedly, there was a small voice in the back of Jack's mind that told him Hayley could be mistaken about seeing the infamous fugitive. But due to her excellent reputation as a bounty hunter and the skills he'd already seen her put into action, he was more inclined to believe in her.

Katherine and Milo had once again made the trek back to Range River and the Eagle Rapids Bail Bonds office to work on the case. They would be there for a good part of the day, dealing with the age-progressed photo as well as making calls and looking through old files related to Ridge that were stored somewhere on one of the office computers.

"You're assuming our happy-couple cover will get blown and we go back to being admitted bounty hunters?" Hayley asked. "And that's when we'll need photos to show people and maybe even post them or hand them out?"

"It's bound to happen eventually," Jack

said. "But it won't be because I can't play the part of a loving husband." He placed his hand atop hers on the table, enjoying the moment as she fixed a tough-girl scowl on her face while her cheeks turned pink.

Hayley looked at Jack's hand lying loosely atop hers. She turned her hand over and gave his a gentle squeeze.

The emotion that passed through Jack was surprising. It felt like the acknowledgment of a growing connection between them that he didn't dare talk about. Because giving voice to it would make it real. And he'd rather pretend it wasn't happening. It was easier that way. He wouldn't get hurt.

When she looked up at him, his heart just about fell out of his chest. The expression in her blue eyes was warm, but also questioning. She wanted to know what he was feeling and he was not about to say. So he just sat there, looking back at her, hoping his own cheeks hadn't turned pink.

"Well, while your people are working on photos, I've got my Range River Bail Bonds office crew doing deep research on Ridge," Hayley said after a moment of silence. Now there was a challenging sparkle in her eyes. "Before you know it, they'll find out Ridge's favorite sports, his shopping and eating habits, hobbies and any other personal information that has come to light in previous investigations. *We* will provide the important detail that leads to his capture."

"With just Jonah and Lorraine working on it at your office?" Jack shook his head. "They're young. They've got a lot to learn."

"They're smart and capable," Hayley said, defending her team. "But I've also got Maribel on it."

"Ah, well, I would expect no less."

From her days working with Connor Ryan at Range River Bail Bonds, Maribel had the research skills and intuition to know what a fugitive might do. She also had connections. A lot of people owed her favors, including other bounty hunters who might be sitting on a piece of information that they'd saved in case they ever got a shot at capturing Ridge.

Jack and Hayley might be working together, but they still had their own individual drives to make this collar. Jack had his own favors and markers to call in, too. And he would use them. Even though the thought tugged at him that the gentlemanly thing to do would be to let Hayley have this capture.

But how could he hold back when Kris

Ridge *had* to be arrested as soon as possible to keep Hayley out of danger? Beyond that, if Jack held back to "let" her win the chase and find Ridge, wouldn't that be an insult to her skills?

"When I finally talked to Connor late last night, he said he had info on where in Range River they'd looked for Kris Ridge in the past," Hayley said. "Residences he'd gone to hoping to spot Ridge, individuals who'd know the fugitive and places where he'd liked to hang out in town. So when Jonah and Lorraine have time, they'll revisit those places and see what they can find out."

"We've got a couple of leads for Katherine and Milo to check on while they're in town, too."

"Oh, really?" Hayley lifted her chin. "Would you have told me about that if I hadn't told you about my potential leads first?"

Jack shrugged. Honestly? He likely wouldn't have.

Wanting to be the best at what he did probably seemed petty to most people. That didn't matter. Jack was compelled to prove his worth. He returned from his overseas tours alive. Some of his buddies had perished over there. He *had* to make his life mean something.

That's what his career was about. Doing something worthwhile with his life. Proving his survival wasn't some kind of mistake. And pursuing that goal—no holds barred—took all of his time and energy.

He looked at Hayley's hand still holding his and thought about what she'd been doing when he'd been overseas while he and his buddies were getting shot at. And he was getting dumped by his wife.

Hayley would have been a kid then.

And smart as she was, tough as she was, well, he knew she wasn't a kid, but she was *young*.

This mild flirtation between the two of them, the one neither one of them wanted to admit to, might be fun for her, but it was dangerous for him. He didn't have the emotional resiliency he'd had when he was twentysomething. And she had the right to be youthful.

Playing at being married was messing with his head. Seeing Hayley late in the evening as they went over the workday, seeing her again in the morning as the four bounty hunters met in the living room to drink coffee and talk about their plans, kept triggering feelings he'd long buried and would like to keep buried. Feelings about family and kids and a future other than living alone.

He'd given up his shot at family life when his marriage failed. In the aftermath, he'd decided to pursue a career and accomplishments instead. And he'd made the most of that decision. Too much time had passed for him to change direction. He was not the kind of man who was going to have his own family.

At some point he and Hayley would make contact with Ridge or somehow be able to prove he was in Blue Mountain. Then Chief Silva would have to call in the feds or do something to help with Ridge's capture. At that point the bounty hunters would be operating more in the open. And this marriage charade would stop.

He withdrew his hand from Hayley's, realizing that in too many ways he'd already let things go too far with her.

They were competitors *temporarily* working together. Once this job was over he'd go back to full-out competition against Range River Bail Bonds and their bounty hunters—including Hayley—because that was how he rolled. It was the life he'd chosen.

Hayley would have a happy life including a romantic future with someone other than him to skip back to when this was all over and Ridge was in custody.

That would be the end of it, because being *friends* with a hotshot bounty hunter who also happened to be Connor Ryan's little sister would be way more headache than Jack would have time for. Especially when he found her so attractive.

"According to everything I checked online, Freedom Motorsports is the busiest motorcycle sales and repair shop in town and it's got the best reviews." Hayley glanced up from her phone and turned to Jack. "Makes as much sense to start here as anywhere."

They were on the sidewalk outside a repurposed redbrick warehouse on the edge of the downtown area. Through the big plate-glass windows, Hayley could see that the forward interior had been turned into a trendy shop with shiny motorcycles on display, along with accessories and racks of biker-related clothing. On their drive around the building before they'd parked, they'd seen open roll-up doors with a view of the repair bays in the back.

"Okay, let's go inside." Jack reached for her hand.

Hayley's heart pumped a little faster when

his fingers touched hers. If she were ruled by common sense, which she felt she normally was, that stir of emotion would not happen. Or she'd be able to will it away. Seemingly countless times she'd told herself that their relationship had nowhere to go—and really, they had no *actual* personal relationship, anyway.

Every time she thought there might be a chance at one, that Jack might want to pursue one, he retreated, and she wondered if she'd just been imagining a closeness he didn't feel.

Barely an hour ago, at breakfast, she'd felt a shift toward coolness in Jack's demeanor. It felt like things had gone back to the way they'd been at the very beginning of their joint venture.

Well, they'd only ever been *pretending* that they had feelings for each other, right? And when she'd given in to that impulse and squeezed his hand, that was only for show, too, right?

*Yeah, sure.*

There wasn't much point in lying to herself. Whether it was smart or not, she'd let herself grow a little bit attached to Jack.

As they walked into the motorcycle shop, she laced her fingers with his. And then she moved closer until they brushed shoulders. She put a smile on her face. They were visiting the shop posing as a happy couple, hoping to establish some sort of friendly relationship with an employee or two. If they had to admit later they were really bounty hunters, they hoped the staff would still be inclined to help them.

Since Ridge had been riding a motorcycle when Hayley saw him, it seemed plausible that he shopped in motorsports stores or had repairs done at shops in town. Until they acquired more background information about him, this felt like the only good option they had.

Jack pulled open the door and they stepped inside.

"Honey, look at this one," Hayley said, leading him toward a big shiny Kawasaki. She made a fuss over it, oohing and aahing.

Jack showed interest and within a few moments a saleswoman walked over to them. Facts about the engine size and capabilities, along with a quick comparison to other motorcycles of similar makes and models, flew out the woman's mouth as she spoke to Hayley.

Hayley smiled in response. "It's a beauty," she finally said.

"Are you specifically looking for a street bike?" the saleswoman asked smoothly. "Or do you like to ride off-road, as well? We've got some fantastic dirt bikes marked down to amazing prices since it's late in the season. Buy one of these and you'll be able to get in a little bit of mud riding before the snow flies."

"Where do people like to go dirt biking around here?" Hayley patted Jack's arm before saying, "My husband and I have just recently arrived in town."

"Ah, well, we've got some fantastic opportunities all over this region. Several of the larger commercial landholders sell season passes that give you access to ride on their property. Tell you what, if you find a couple of dirt bikes you like at these low prices, I'll throw in the passes for the rest of this season and for the next season starting in spring, as well."

Under other circumstances, Hayley might have been put off by the woman's hard-sale tactics. But at the moment, she couldn't help appreciating someone just trying to do their job. Because she was just trying to do her job, too.

"Do you have any good riding clubs around here?" Hayley asked as she followed the saleswoman toward the dirt bikes with Jack trailing behind. "My husband here knows what he's doing, but I could use some lessons. And, well, it would be fun to meet people."

"Of course!" Sensing a potential sale, the woman immediately led the way to a bulletin board with a couple of flyers for riding events on it. Hayley took pictures to get the contact information. The woman then went on to mention a couple of social media accounts linked to groups where Hayley and Jack could meet up with local riders.

Hayley exchanged a slight smile with Jack. This bundle of potential contacts was exactly what they'd wanted. They hoped to catch Ridge quickly, but connecting with some of these local motorcycle riders could be helpful if the chase started to drag out.

While Hayley talked to the saleswoman, she watched Jack make his way to the parts-and-repairs service counter where he chatted with a man in a work shirt and wearing safety glasses.

They left a short time later with Hayley carrying a handful of glossy motorcycle sales flyers. "If Ridge is hiding out this close to Range River, do you think he's stayed in contact with anybody there?" she asked Jack.

His answer was drowned out by the roar of an accelerating engine coming up on the street beside them. And then, *Bang! Bang! Bang!*

The first two bullets whizzed past Hayley's shoulder and burst through the window of the yarn supply shop beside her. Shattered glass, like a sharp-edged waterfall, rained onto the sidewalk. With the sound of the third shot, Hayley felt a tug forward as she and Jack dropped down to the pavement and sought cover from the shooter behind a parked car.

"Kris Ridge!" Hayley hissed out the name despite the assailant's face being hidden by his full helmet with face screen. Who else could it be?

Heart thundering in her chest and her body tensed with fear, she made herself take a couple of steadying breaths. And then, still crouched, she darted toward the front of the car that was sheltering them, determined to get a good look at the motorcycle as the assailant sped away. She hoped to get a glimpse of some distinctive characteristic or at least part of the license plate number. But she was too late. Too quickly, the rider turned a corner and disappeared from sight. It looked like the same motorcycle she'd seen Ridge on last night, but she wouldn't be able to tell the police any more about it than that.

"You all right?" Jack asked, moving up alongside her, both of them standing, now.

"I'm fine." Disappointment in herself for not responding faster came out in her annoyed tone.

Shoppers on both sides of the street who had ducked into stores or dropped to the pavement to get out of the line of fire began to cautiously reappear or get to their feet.

"Are you *certain* you weren't hit?" Jack demanded, reaching to grab a section of Hayley's jacket and showing her a hole that hadn't been there before.

Hayley felt the blood drain from her face. That sensation of being tugged forward had been a bullet ripping into her jacket. *Had* she been hit? Had fear and adrenaline made her oblivious to her injury?

Steeling herself for the worst, she unzipped her jacket and looked down, expecting to see blood. She didn't. A sigh of relief escaped her and she dropped her tensed shoulders. Her hands still shook, though. That gunshot had come way too close, passing through the section of her unzipped jacket that had been hanging open rather than actually hitting her body. *Thank You, Lord.*

A chilling scream jolted her rapidly beating heart before it had a chance to calm down. Hayley turned toward the sound.

Several steps ahead on the sidewalk, a woman lay on the concrete with a circle of blood blossoming in the center of her blouse. A second woman knelt beside her, hand over her mouth, apparently the one who had screamed.

"Call an ambulance!" Jack sprinted toward the injured woman.

Hayley tapped the emergency icon on her screen and then stepped back from the buildings to look for street numbers and store names so she could give the dispatcher a better description of where they were.

Standing on the curb, she heard the roar of a motorcycle engine again and turned.

Ridge was back, and this time he was driving straight at her.

She reached for her gun, but there were too many people around for her to risk taking a shot. Unwilling to put innocents in further danger, Hayley released her grip on her gun and sprinted across the street.

The sound of rubber sliding on pavement and gravel told her the motorcyclist had hit the brakes and spun to accelerate again in her direction. Within seconds she heard the grind of the engine catching up with her.

Gasping for breath as fear gripped her lungs, she darted around the edge of an office building and down what she assumed was an alley leading to the next street. She'd assumed wrong. It was a dead end. A small parking area, with the office building on one side and brick walls on the other two. Without looking she knew Ridge followed her into what she now realized was a trap, as the sound of the motorcycle's powerful engine bounced off the surrounding walls.

With a brick wall in front of her, Hayley could run no farther. This time she did pull her gun from her holster, and she whipped around, ready to fight for her life.

The motorcyclist stopped just a few feet away from her.

Her dry throat burned as she breathed and her palms were sweating.

The motorcyclist braked and then grabbed the gun holstered at his waist. Hayley took aim, but then a flash of movement behind him caught her eye. A couple of kids on skateboards had rolled up on the sidewalk behind the motorcyclist and stopped to gawk.

They weren't directly in her line of fire, but they were close enough. A wide shot or a ricocheted bullet, either of them could get the kids injured or killed.

From the corner of her eye she glimpsed the dark green color of an industrial trash container pressed up against one of the brick walls with various pieces of junk and refuse piled around it. Adrenaline-fueled fear had her thinking she could make a run for it and use it to leap up and over the wall.

In front of her the assailant stood, straddling the motorcycle, and lifting both hands to take aim at her. "You think you're going to be the one who captures me?" Even over the loud rumbling of the idle engine, she could recognize Kris Ridge's voice. "You're not. Nobody will." He fired.

Hayley dived to her right, desperate to get to the end of the container, hoping its steel frame would give her some protection. She couldn't see Ridge from the spot where she crouched on the filthy asphalt, but she heard the motorcycle moving again. Her plan to climb onto the container and jump over the wall was useless now. She would be an easy target if she tried.

Frantic, she looked around the pile of junk

on the ground beside her, desperate to find a weapon that wouldn't endanger the boys who could still be close by. There was a busted-up wooden pallet beside her and she grabbed a chunk of it. Ridge inched his motorcycle around the trash container. Hayley lunged at him with the piece of weathered boards and rusted nails, flailing at his unprotected arms and shoulders.

In his right hand, Ridge awkwardly held on to both his gun and the handlebar. Hayley aimed for that vulnerable spot, whacking as hard as she could. He lost his grip on the weapon and it clattered to the ground.

As he reached for it, she managed to hit him again on the back of the neck. He lurched forward, but immediately recovered and turned to swing a punch at her. She dodged and managed to avoid the brunt of the hit, but his fist clipped on the side of her jaw, sending her stumbling backward until she tripped and fell.

She pushed herself back to her feet in time to see him grab his gun, make a tight U-turn, fire one more shot in her direction, which missed, and then accelerate out to the road and speed away.

As soon as he was gone she heard the approaching sirens of emergency vehicles. Maybe that was what scared him away. Either he'd somehow heard the sirens, or he just realized he'd hung around his crime scene too long.

Hayley was grateful whatever the reason, and offered up a silent prayer of gratitude as Jack appeared on the sidewalk and then raced up the short passageway. When he reached her, he wrapped his arms around her and held her tight. She could feel his heart beating nearly as quickly as hers. "I'll be all right," she said, though she still felt very shaky after nearly losing her life. "What about the woman you were helping?"

"I finally got her friend calmed down enough to put pressure on her wound so I could come help you." He still hadn't loosened his hold on her.

"Ridge spoke to me," Hayley said. "It was definitely him. I recognized his voice from some of the old news videos we watched."

Jack slowly loosened his embrace and took hold of her hands. "What did he say?"

"That I wasn't going to catch him. Nobody would. But he was wrong."

Jack squeezed her hands and sighed. "I was afraid he would target you."

Blue and red lights flashed in their direction as police pulled up to the scene.

"I'm not thrilled about it, either." Hayley offered him a tired half smile. "But he's a dangerous man to have loose on the streets. We need to track him down and take him into custody."

# TEN

"What's your best guess on what the topic of this meeting will be?" Hayley asked Jack.

He turned in response to her questions as they walked up the steps to the Blue Mountain police department's public entrance. "I'm hoping that after the attack on you this morning he's going to tell us that he's now pulling out all the stops to find Kris Ridge."

Chief Silva had sent a text directing them to show up at his office. At the scene of the attack outside Freedom Motorsports that morning the chief had been exceptionally busy. Hayley and Jack had given their statements, but there'd been no opportunity to talk about coordinating their efforts to find Ridge now that the chief was convinced the fugitive really was in his town.

"Do you think one or more of the local cops could be on the take?" Hayley asked quietly. "And maybe that's why Ridge has been able to hide out here?"

"Don't know. What I do think is that if Kris Ridge is found here in Blue Mountain, and it turns out he's been here for years, local law enforcement is going to look bad. Even if they weren't corrupt, they would still look inept. Even if holding that opinion was unfair. People don't always want to see the truth uncovered. Especially if it might embarrass them."

Jack reached for the door and at the same time heard a voice call out his name. He turned to see Virgil Agnew, bundled up for the cooler weather, cutting across the narrow lawn in front of the building and heading toward them. "Good afternoon." He turned to Hayley. "How are you holding up?"

"I'm still alive. And I intend to stay that way."

Jack's heart sped up a little as he listened to her determined words. The more he was around her, the more he noticed how vibrant she was. Everyone else seemed dull in comparison.

That was a problem. He thought he could work closely with her for a few days, pretend to be married for the sake of the job and then walk away unscathed. He wasn't so sure about that now. Thoughts of her and how she'd looked at particular moments when she was smiling or serious or brave, like she was right now, stuck in his mind and didn't want to let go.

But she was young, with a lot of hope and resiliency still within her. He was older, somewhat embittered, and he wanted to stay that way. Even if he didn't feel like he wanted to let go of those thoughts of her and how she was starting to make him feel, he had to. For both their sakes.

They walked inside the building where Jack let the desk officer know that he and Hayley were there for a meeting with Silva.

"I'm here to meet with him, too," Agnew said from behind Jack. "I just got a text asking me to come down here."

"Same for us," Hayley told him.

The senior lawman raised his silvery eyebrows. "Well, it'll be interesting to see what this is about."

They were briskly escorted back to the chief's office. Parker was already waiting there. Silva stood to greet the new arrivals before inviting them to have a seat in the visitor chairs. "How are you doing?" he asked Hayley while everyone was getting situated.

"I'm okay," she said. "And more than ready

to capture Ridge so we can wrap this up. I'm tired of people trying to kill me."

"I can understand that."

The chief was looking tired, Jack noted. And stressed. Markedly different from how he'd appeared when the bounty hunters first came into town.

"So, I asked the three of you to drop by for several reasons," Silva started. "First, I want you to know that Foster's two partners in crime have already turned on him. I've heard from the prosecutor's office down in Range River that Peter Hofer and Lee Weser have both agreed to trade information for lesser charges."

"That's not exactly great news," Hayley said, disappointment evident in her voice. "Those two jerks nearly killed Luther and tried really hard to kill me and the rest of our crew."

"They better not walk," Jack said, as angry as Hayley was at the news. "They need to be kept off the streets."

"It's how the legal system works." Silva gave Hayley and Jack a lingering look. "I wish things were different, too. But we've got to work with what we have. And what we have so far is the both of them claiming that

Foster was the one who shot Luther. Beyond that they're also claiming that he started the cabin fire and he was the only one who shot into the cabin."

"And you believe them?" Hayley demanded. "I don't. All three of them are guilty."

"Yeah, well, passing judgment on them within the legal system isn't my job. And it isn't your job, either. Eventually they'll all get their day in court." He leaned back in his chair. "The good news is that it does wrap up our open investigations regarding the three of them."

"Has anybody asked Foster about Kris Ridge?" Hayley tapped her cowboy-booted toe on the floor, looking impatient. "This could be the perfect situation to discover the connection between them."

Silva exchanged glances with Parker before turning back to Hayley. "Actually, that leads to another of the reasons why I asked you two, and Virgil, to come in and talk to me." He leaned back in his chair. "We haven't made any headway on finding the motorcyclist who attacked you this morning. You said it was Kris Ridge, that you were certain of it, and at this point I'm beginning to believe you."

"Finally." Hayley stopped toe-tapping and leaned forward. "So what's the plan?"

"While my officers continue to investigate the two attacks on you, I want the three of you to focus solely on locating Ridge. If you really think he's out there, that he's your attacker, then fine, our investigations overlap." He turned to the former chief. "Virgil, I want you to use all your old informants, connections, whatever resources you have, to help find him."

Agnew nodded. "I'd very much like to do that."

"Meanwhile, I'll work with the prosecutor down in Range River. See if she can offer some kind of incentive to Foster so he'll tell us how he's connected to Ridge and what he knows about him."

"We can't assume Ridge is moving around like some kind of lone wolf." Hayley rubbed her fingers over her chin.

"He got away with gold coins that he needed to convert into cash. Maybe he's stayed off the radar for so long because he's been liquidating those assets slowly, and he had to pay people off to do it, maybe by offering a percentage of his ultimate take. Those people could be watching out for him."

And those same people could be willing to do whatever it took to silence Hayley if they wanted to protect their gains.

Jack's phone chimed. He'd received a text from Katherine, an age-progressed photo of Ridge attached.

He showed it to Hayley.

"Yeah, that's close," she said. "But there are a few adjustments that need to be made."

Jack handed his phone to Silva, who looked at the photo and then handed the phone to Agnew.

Agnew held on to the phone the longest, staring at the pictures. "I hate to think he could have been here all the years that I was chief and I was clueless about it." He shook his head. Then he looked up with a bit of fire in his eyes. "Makes me mad."

"Will you forward me that picture?" Agnew asked.

"Of course."

Jack sent the photo to everyone in the room.

"Do you have any specific places in mind regarding where you're going to look for Ridge?" Hayley asked Agnew.

"I know which bars the town's hard cases like to hang around in, so maybe I'll start with them. It's been a while since I've done anything undercover. It'll be fun for the old police chief to see if he can slip in unnoticed. For starters I'll just hang out and eavesdrop. See if there's any unusual energy or chatter. I don't think it's likely I'd actually see Ridge, but you never know."

"I've got somebody at my bail bond agency doing research and putting together a dossier that I should have by this evening," Hayley said to him. "That should give us some idea of the specific kinds of places where we should look for him based on habits and known preferences."

"Katherine and Milo are working on something similar," Jack added. "We're going to compile everything—" he hesitated, looking at Hayley and waiting for a nod of acknowledgment, which she gave him "—and then we'll put together more specific plans."

"I think the best thing for us right now would be to head back to the area around Carriage Street." Hayley glanced at Jack and he nodded in agreement. "We could drive along the side street he was on before he rode up to the intersection where I saw him. Maybe we'll be able to spot some outside security cameras. He wears a helmet so we're not going to get an image of his face, but maybe we can get his license plate number."

The computer on Silva's desk chimed and he glanced at the screen. "I've got to wrap this up. I've got a meeting to attend."

"Ah, yes," Agnew said. "The seemingly never-ending meetings. How well I remember those."

Everyone exchanged goodbyes and Jack and Hayley started down the hallway toward the exit.

Agnew caught up with them. "You two be careful," he said as all three of them walked out the door. "You, especially," he said to Hayley. "Ridge doesn't want to go back to prison and he's afraid you could make that happen. So far you're the only one of us who's actually seen him and knows for a fact that he's in town. Scared people do desperate things. It's risky for him to draw attention to himself like this, but my guess is he's going to want to shut you up and then fade back into the woodwork, with everyone left wondering whether you actually ever saw him or not."

"I'll be careful," Hayley assured him.

They were just about to part ways when the former chief paused for a moment and scratched his gray beard. "You didn't ask for my advice, but I'm just going to go ahead and suggest you hold off trying to physically apprehend Ridge if you find him. Tell Silva where he is and then let the cops do the takedown. I realize it would be a big payday if you captured him, but it might not be worth it. He'll fight hard, figuring he has nothing to lose." Agnew adjusted his glasses. "My wife passed away eight months before I retired. She fought her illness for a long time." He nodded to himself. "Life is precious. Hers certainly was. You need to do everything you can to protect it. And that includes protecting your own lives."

"We'll be careful," Hayley assured him.

"No way we're calling the cops to take down Ridge if we find him," Jack said when they got into his truck.

"Agreed," Hayley said. "I imagine when we get to Agnew's age we'll think more like him, but right now, I just want to get our fugitive."

"Me, too."

"But we're not doing anything unethical or illegal to capture him," she added.

Disappointment settled on Jack's shoulders. Hayley still thought he was unethical. He supposed he shouldn't be surprised. But he had gotten his hopes up with Hayley, a little. Despite his determination to keep his distance, he still allowed himself to care about her as someone more than just a temporary work partner. And he'd hoped that she would think better of him than that.

"Have you ever seen me do some terrible thing in the course of our working together that would make you think I was a thug?" he asked, unable to set aside his annoyance.

"No," she said. "Not yet."

"So why would you assume I lack ethical standards? Because you heard people gossip about me?"

They rode toward Carriage Street in silence.

"You know, I have to say I haven't seen you work in any way that wasn't professional," she finally said. "I'm sorry I believed the gossip."

"Apology accepted."

He turned onto Margaret Avenue and headed toward the intersection with Carriage Street. Along the way they passed a coffee stand, a consignment store, a crafts shop and a scattering of other small businesses. None of them appeared to have outside security cameras pointed toward the street.

When they reached the actual intersection where Hayley had seen Ridge, Jack turned onto Carriage Street and then pulled to the curb.

One of the most frustrating aspects of

bounty hunting was having bits of information that wouldn't make any sense until you got that one final piece that tied everything all together.

"Why would Ridge have been here right at the perfect moment to intercept Foster?" Jack asked.

"They must have been in communication," Hayley said. "That's the only thing I can think of."

"Is it any clearer to you now whether Ridge was trying to help Foster escape or trying to get him caught?"

"No." She shook her head. "I feel like there's a bigger picture here and we just aren't seeing it."

Jack agreed. And it might mean that there was a danger to Hayley that they weren't seeing, too.

"I printed a few copies of the age-progressed photo of Kris Ridge you approved." Katherine walked into the suite at the Bear's Lair Lodge and extended a file folder toward Hayley.

"Thanks." Hayley took a look inside. They'd decided to work with the original booking photo because it offered the clearest image.

And right now she was looking at the face that matched the one she'd seen nearly twenty-four hours ago and recognized as the infamous fugitive.

Hayley and Jack had eaten lunch after their drive down Margaret Avenue earlier in the day, and then returned to the same area on the off chance that they'd see something they could develop into a lead. Because at that point they had nothing.

They did find a convenience store at the end of the avenue farthest from the Carriage Street intersection and it had outdoor security cameras, but the manager wouldn't even consider allowing them to look at any of their recent footage. "Come back with a cop and a warrant" had been his final word before he turned and walked away from them.

At that point they'd headed back to the lodge to search the social media accounts for the motorcycle groups the saleswoman had told them about.

"You'd think he would have been wearing colored contacts to disguise his heterochromia when you saw him," Katherine said, looking over Hayley's shoulder at the photo.

"Could be he's gotten lazy." Milo set a computer case and satchel on the coffee table.

"Or arrogant. At this point he's probably sure he's smarter than anyone looking for him."

Katherine walked away and Jack stepped up beside Hayley to look at the picture even though all of the bounty hunters had already seen the digital version.

"Light brown and medium green eyes don't look that radically different from each other," he said after a moment. "I don't know if the difference would be so noticeable if you weren't a cop or bounty hunter and used to memorizing distinctive characteristics."

Milo pulled his laptop out of its case and situated it in front of him as he sat on the couch, Katherine sat beside him, and Hayley and Jack settled into chairs opposite them.

"First off, I promise to not read aloud everything in the files. I know that drives you crazy," Milo said with a glance at Jack. "I printed a hard copy because phone connectivity and Wi-Fi here can be so iffy and we've included a fair number of images."

Jack had his tablet out. He'd tried to open the attachments but it was taking forever. Finally he reached for the printed version. Hayley got up and moved her chair closer so that she could look over the report alongside him.

"Did you contact Maribel and see if she had anything to add?" Hayley asked.

Katherine grinned. "She very politely told us that she'd sent you an email and that *you* could decide if you wanted to share that information with us."

"Of course." It struck Hayley how comfortable she'd gotten working with "the competition." Did the rest of her team feel the same way? Maybe not so much.

She reached for her phone, scanned for an email from Maribel and read through the brief message.

"Looks like she's collected some random bits of personal information about Ridge," she said. "She got the information from Connor's files plus a few bounty hunter friends who were willing to help her out."

"Did the bounty hunters ask *why* she wanted the information?" Jack glanced up from the stack of papers in his hand to look at Hayley. "I would have. And I would have kept the information to myself until she told me specifically where Ridge had been sighted. After that I would have shared everything I had, because I want him off the streets, but I also would have gone after him myself."

That was typical Jack. Competitive.

But not unethical. Maribel, a member of Hayley's team, had been reluctant to share too much information, too.

The fact was, Hayley wasn't all that different from him.

She glanced at Jack beside her, contemplating her earlier concern about his business ethics. She liked to think of herself as someone who disavowed gossip and focused her attention on facts and behavior that she personally witnessed.

For the sake of her job she was usually pretty observant. But when it came to Jack, her vision became murky. She kept looking for a reason to dislike and distrust him. She didn't want to get too attached. And yet, since the morning after they'd captured Foster, when she'd felt Jack emotionally distance himself after she'd held his hand at breakfast, she'd felt the loss of something important between them.

No, she hadn't. That was ridiculous. *Get yourself together.* She shook her head slightly. The intense focus and teamwork of a manhunt brought people together temporarily. *Just temporarily.* There was no substance to it. There couldn't be.

She found her gaze drawn to Jack. Sitting there sprawled in the chair, looking like anything but a sympathetic character. And yet when you thought about his career over the years, he'd helped a lot of people. It had to bother a man of integrity to realize so many people thought the worst of him. For no real reason.

And she'd been one of those people.

"Anybody else hungry?" Katherine asked. "Because I'm starving. I'm going to need some brain food before we discuss the notes and plan our next steps."

"I second that," Milo said.

"Go ahead and get dinner." Jack's tablet had finally finished opening the attachments, so he handed the printed version to Hayley. "I'm anxious to look over everything. Just bring me something back. Anything's fine."

"I'm going to stay here, too," Hayley said. There was no way she'd let Jack get ahead of her on reviewing the information. "And I'm not a picky eater, either." She forwarded Maribel's email to the other three bounty hunters.

The lodge didn't offer room service, but Katherine and Milo could pick up meals downstairs and bring them to the suite. They left, talking amiably to each other as Hayley went back to reading notes.

"It says here that Ridge liked to shoot pool,"

she said a short time later. "That he played in tournaments and generally liked to fleece people in pool halls if he could get them to place bets. There are several notes in here that indicate he liked to be seen appearing smarter than other people. That probably hasn't changed."

Jack looked over at her.

It would seem obvious to most people that a person on the run would cut out human contact as much as possible and try to remain isolated. Some fugitives did, at the beginning. Most ended up getting bored or lonesome over time. Then, like anybody else, they'd get back out into the social mix and return to their old habits.

"I think we should check out some of the pool halls they have here in Blue River tonight after we eat," she continued. "Look around, talk to people. Do our married couple checking out the town routine. See if we can make friends with the employees. I don't think we should show his picture around just yet. It's one thing to mention rumors of a famous fugitive possibly being in town. It's another thing altogether to flash around an age-progressed photo of him. We could inadvertently show it to a friend of his who would alert him and he'd take off."

"Good idea." Jack nodded. "And I agree, it makes sense to hold off on the picture until it no longer pays to be stealthy and we're ready to put the pressure on Ridge and chase him publicly. Ideally, I'd want to have the police on our side before we do that. Which means we're going to have to come up with some kind of proof to show Chief Silva."

Hayley grabbed her phone. "I'm going to call Agnew. He should have some ideas on which bars attract people who want to shoot pool."

She placed the call and Agnew gave her a half-dozen suggestions. Jack tapped the names and locations into his tablet as Hayley repeated them. The former chief still had his own plans to hit a few bars later in the night to see if he could pick up any information— or even rumors—about Ridge being in town.

Katherine and Milo returned shortly with dinner, juggling a pitcher of iced tea and bags of take-out containers that they set on the small dinette table.

While the four of them ate, Hayley summarized the plan that she and Jack had for the evening. "We can review all the notes and work on a broader strategic plan to find Ridge in the morning," she said. "Right now Jack and I want to go out and *do* something."

Katherine laughed and then shook her head. "I'd expect no less from either of you." Her smile slowly faded. "Would you like Milo and me to go with you?"

Hayley thought for a moment. "If we had limitless resources, I'd say yes. But we're just taking a shot in the dark with this. It could end up being time wasted. Instead of going with us, why don't you pick up where we left off on the motorcycle club social media accounts? Finish scrolling through and searching for anybody who looks like Ridge. Maybe even search through some local pool tournament social media pages, too, while you're at it."

Katherine glanced at her boss for his input.

"I agree," he said. "We can't afford to waste time. Chances are slim that we'll get anything substantial accomplished tonight, but as we all know, it's often the small pieces of information that eventually add up and send us in the right direction."

"I'm all for heading in the right direction," Milo muttered.

"Me, too," Jack agreed with a glance at Hayley. "Because I'm sure Ridge isn't just hoping that Hayley will fade away. He's going to be making plans to silence her, and we need to get ahead of that.

# ELEVEN

"Looks like the rain is setting in for a while." Hayley gazed at the steady drops falling in front of her and the puddles on the pavement reflecting the red and green and blue neon lights shining from the building behind her.

"Give it another week or two and it will be falling as snow." Jack tilted his head back to look up at the low clouds.

They'd just come out of a bar called Corner Pocket and were now standing on the narrow walkway in front of the building, pausing beneath the roof's overhang. It was the last bar on the list of venues Agnew had given them. They hadn't gotten any notable reaction from anyone when they mentioned Kris Ridge, and of course they hadn't seen him there. Hayley had anticipated the evening would turn out like that. But still, she'd let herself get her hopes up so she was disappointed. At least they had gotten a list of dates and times for the pool-shooting tournaments the bar hosted. That might be a reason to check back there in the future. They'd also gotten information on related social media accounts.

Looking up at the low clouds, she drew in a damp breath, exhaled and watched the resulting vapor drift away in foggy wisps. "Feels good to be out in fresh air," she said, thinking not only about the dank interior of the bar, but also back to that horrible feeling of being trapped in the cabin fire.

"And it's quiet." Jack turned to her. "I'd rather listen to the sound of falling rain than loud bar music any day. But then I'm an old man, right?" He smiled. "A cranky one, I suppose."

The funny thing was, she'd rather listen to raindrops, too. Well, some of the time. Did that make her old, as well?

Somewhere over the past few days, as they'd spent nearly all their waking hours together, she'd stopped thinking of Jack as older. The difference in their ages was a fact. One that she believed would create a significant divide between them. But after working a case alongside him while they pretended to be husband and wife, she'd found that the age difference didn't divide them at all. They were decidedly different people in some regards, but most of the time they were able to meet in the middle when it came to significant decisions. They'd melded together easily. Like...*actual* married people did.

Her stomach took a jolt when she realized the turn her thoughts had taken.

She was *not* married to him. She did not want to *be* married to him.

The very idea was crazy.

Wasn't it?

Until she'd worked with him, in fact, she'd not thought about marriage much at all except to hope and pray it happened for her sometime in the future. She had a great job and was making a name for herself.

She just figured one day she'd meet the right person and make it all work.

What if the right person was standing next to her all along?

"At your advanced years you should be thankful that you can even hear raindrops and loud music," she said, desperate to return to believing that he was simply too old for her and that was the end of it.

He laughed. "The funny thing is, I do thank God every day for a lot of things. Being physically strong and healthy is near the top of my list."

She tilted her head. "Seriously? You're a praying man?"

She'd never thought about him having a faith life. It surprised her to realize that.

"I'm not trying to pass myself off as perfect," he said, a slight smile on his lips. "But I do lean into my faith to get through life and do my job. To help me do my best to assist people when I can whether they appreciate it or not."

It was an honest, unpretentious statement and Hayley's heart melted just a little.

*No. No, no, no! I am not going there!*

This was a *job*. Whatever personal relationship they had was pretend. She had to keep telling herself that.

"I am sincerely glad to know that you are a person of faith," she said after a few moments, trying to make sure that her conflicting feelings didn't somehow slip out in her tone of voice or the way she looked at him. Because knowing this now made him that much more attractive. "I suppose it does show in your actions that you do possess a scrap of character." She smiled at him to soften her attempt at a joke.

Instead of taking offense, he laughed. "I suppose that depends on who you ask."

If someone asked her, what would she say about him?

She couldn't help focusing on the lines around his eyes when he smiled. They were endearing. So at the moment, if someone asked her, she would have to describe him as distracting.

She shook her head to clear her thoughts. Not the right time or place for that line of thought.

Determined to return her focus to their manhunt, Hayley hooked a thumb and jerked it back to indicate the bar behind them. "Do you think it would be worth our time to check a few more bars? We've got about three more hours until closing time."

"We did what we set out to do. For now, I think it would be more worthwhile to head back to the lodge and see if Milo and Katherine have found anything helpful on social media. Or better yet, if they found some connection between Ridge and Barry Foster."

What he said made sense. Hayley had wanted to visit a few more bars just because she was anxious to *do* something that would help them capture Ridge. But there were times when a smart strategy was better than action.

"Your advanced age must be making you tired," she teased. "That's why you want to head back to the lodge."

Jack held her gaze, the corner of his mouth quirking upward in a half smile. "Despite what people think, bounty hunting is not just a knuckle-dragging chase. It's oftentimes a thinking game. But *kids* like you don't usually have the mental strength to handle that."

She laughed. How could she be offended when she'd started it?

What did get under her skin, though, was the realization that for some silly reason she didn't want him to think of her as a kid.

Forget the appearance and shallow ego aspects that sometimes went along with people worrying about their age. That wasn't her concern. Hayley had had an unusual childhood. She'd faced tragedy and loss at an early age when her parents were killed in a car accident. She liked to believe that as a result of her experiences, she'd developed some maturity and depth of character. At least she hoped she had.

"All right." She nodded. "Let's head back to the lodge."

Jack flipped up the collar on his jacket. "Excellent example of mature judgment."

They splashed their way through the puddles in the parking lot to Jack's truck, got in and started driving back toward the stretch of town along the eastern edge of Peregrine Lake where the lodge was located.

There was a little bit of late-night traffic, but it thinned as they headed away from the main downtown area. Hayley idly watched the headlights of the oncoming cars, then shifted her gaze toward the lights from the homes and businesses alongside the road until they thinned out, too. Soon the road would rise in elevation, hugging a section of mountainside on the east end of the lake.

Kris Ridge might have bolted when Hayley recognized him, but Hayley felt like he was probably still somewhere in this town. Especially if he'd been living here under everyone's noses for fifteen years. Obviously using an identity other than his own. Despite his horrible behavior, the man was human. He would feel a connection to Blue Mountain after being here for so long. He likely had friends, maybe even a wife and some kids. He wouldn't want to just run off if he believed simply killing Hayley would secure the life he enjoyed.

Ridge's haul from the robbery had never been recovered. How had he sold it—or was he waiting for the right buyer, the right moment? Ridge could take the money and purchase a false identity and then use it to buy a house. Or even a business. He could potentially hide more successfully if he chose to blend in and have a visible means of financial support rather than being a hermit who lived in a shack in the forest.

Hayley opened her phone, and once again looked over Maribel's email with the list of Ridge's known interests, quirks and habits.

"Ridge's competitive streak doesn't just lend itself to shooting pool," she said to Jack after a moment. "It includes motocross racing, as well. At least it did." She glanced at Jack. "That compulsion to look smart and triumph over other people is how we're going to be able to draw him out somehow. Maybe we could—"

*Bam!*

The sudden jolt of the truck as it was struck from behind knocked the phone out of Hayley's grasp and it clattered to the floorboard.

Surprisingly, the airbags didn't deploy.

The cabin of the truck was lit by the bright headlights that had suddenly appeared behind them. Gauging by their height and intensity, the vehicle they were attached to appeared to be a commercial-size truck. Hayley glanced at her side mirror but the illumination and glare made it impossible for her to see it.

*"What is happening?"* She barely got the words out before a second jolt, this one feeling like it had come at an angle rather from directly behind, struck the rear bumper on the driver's side. As if the intention were to set Jack's truck spinning to the right. That would make it a deadly maneuver. Because if they veered off the right side of the road, they would sail over the edge of a rocky cliff and tumble down a hundred feet into the lake below.

Jack steered quickly, trying to keep his truck on the road.

The glaring headlights behind them began to fade. The driver was backing off.

But then the lights suddenly got brighter again.

"He's coming back," Jack called out. "Brace for another hit."

The driver who was determined to knock them off the cliff had chosen the perfect stretch of road. There were segments of low guardrail, but there were also gaps between them. Jack had taken an assortment of defensive and offensive driver training courses, but none of the practice scenarios exactly matched the situation he now found himself in.

Rain, still pouring down, formed streamlets that followed the slight angle of the road toward the lake. If his truck were struck again at just the right angle, the water flowing across the road would be one more element that could help send them over the edge.

He couldn't gun the engine in an attempt to speed away. If he did that, he risked losing control in one of the turns and veering off and over the edge of the cliff. He didn't dare move into the opposite lane in an attempt to get away from the attacking vehicle, either, because the road hugged the mountainside and he wouldn't be able to see anyone coming toward him on the winding road.

*Lord, protect us!*

He had to take the initiative and do *something*.

The lights behind them flared brighter and the scream of the assailant truck's engine grew shriller as the driver accelerated.

Up ahead, the headlights on Jack's truck shone on a short gap between sections of guardrail, where the low barrier ended and there was a segment of mud and grass before the rail resumed.

The stretch of grass between the edge of the road and the edge of the cliff was narrow. Given the momentum of Jack's truck as he drove, it wasn't exactly a safe option for him to pull over there. If he slammed on his brakes, he might slide atop the water and mud and shoot over the edge of the cliff before he could stop.

Not a great option, but what was his alternative?

Sometimes there was no good alternative. Only a choice that was a little less likely to get you killed.

"I'm going to pull over at that gap up ahead," Jack said. "Be ready for anything."

He lifted his foot from the accelerator as they reached the spot where he intended to stop. At that moment, the assailant truck struck them again.

Jack's truck lurched as he steered hard to the right.

In an instant the world was spinning around him. Objects fell that just moments ago had been in the console beside him. His phone. A travel mug. His tablet.

He saw a whirling image of tree and mountainside and road, all of them seeming to be in the wrong place until his airbag deployed, blocking his view.

*"Jack!"*

Hearing Hayley yell his name, Jack fought around the deployed airbag to reach out his right hand and grab hold of her arm.

The rolling sensation finally stopped, with the truck now right side up.

But it was still moving, sliding slowly across the rain-slickened grass toward the edge of the narrow edge of ground and the sudden drop at the end.

"We've got to get out," Hayley said sharply.

The airbags were deflating. Jack could see Hayley grappling to unlatch her seat belt. He let go of her upper arm so he could unlatch his own. Then he reached for her again, because the truck was moving in her direction. If she opened her door and jumped out, she would get struck by the sliding vehicle. He was going to have to pull her across the console and out the door on his side.

He flung open his door. "This way!" he called out. "I've got you."

Hayley crawled up onto the center console.

Jack grabbed her upper arms, pulled her close and then together they took a tumble out of the truck. Jack tucked in his arms and legs, doing his best to cage Hayley's body while also attempting to land on his hip and shoulder and then roll to help absorb some of the energy of the impact.

The rainwater and mud softened the blow of their landing, and they rolled to a stop.

Slowly, they untangled from one another.

"Are you okay?" Jack asked, reaching out to brush Hayley's wet hair aside so he could see her face.

She nodded. "I think so."

His head was still spinning as he sat up and then looked over toward the road, hoping to see that the attacking vehicle had driven on by.

It hadn't. The truck that had battered them was parked there, its engine running. In the light cast by the headlights, Jack could see someone standing outside the truck, looking in Jack and Hayley's direction as if trying to see what had happened.

A car traveling from the opposite direction drove by and in the wash of its headlights Jack could see confirmation of what he had suspected. "The truck driver is Kris Ridge."

"I see him, too," Hayley said as the car continued by. "But I don't think he realizes we can see him. Let's get him!"

Jack got to his feet and started moving

through the mud, his steps staggering at first as his dizziness cleared.

He knew the precise moment Ridge spotted him because the fugitive turned and ran down the road in the darkness, leaving the idling truck behind. Rain was still coming down. Jack rushed as fast as he could until he reached a section of road that turned away from the mountainside. The flatter ground there was covered with trees, and Ridge could have gone in any direction.

With no indication of which way the murderer, thief and bail jumper had gone, Jack came to a stop.

Hayley ran up beside him, limping slightly.

They heard sirens headed in their direction. Maybe the people who'd driven by in the car didn't want to stop when they'd seen evidence of a crash, but apparently they had called the police.

Jack flagged down the patrol car. The ambulance that had been following pulled up behind it.

"Contact Chief Silva!" Jack said between breaths, and then he gave the officer the tale, leaving out Kris Ridge's name.

When he saw the paramedics walking their way, he heard Hayley telling the emergency medical responders they were all right. She gave Jack a glance and raised her eyebrows. He nodded, signaling he was fine with no treatment.

The officer ran the license plate number on the abandoned commercial truck through his computer. It didn't come back as stolen, but he requested that Dispatch contact the registered owner to find out if it might have been taken and no one had realized it yet.

It wasn't long before Chief Silva arrived on scene.

"It was Ridge," Jack said while going over the details of the incident. "I *saw* him. I chased him but he got away."

"I saw him, too," Hayley added. "I think he figured this was a way to take me out and have it look like an accident on a rainy night. Or an act of random road rage. Something that wouldn't make it obvious he was involved."

Silva breathed out a heavy sigh. "I can see that this crash wasn't an accident. But don't get set on a full-out manhunt for Kris Ridge." He held up his hand when Hayley tried to interrupt him. "I'm going to investigate this like I normally would. That means starting with a visit to the truck's owner. If it turns out the vehicle was stolen, we'll look for a suspect—whoever that might be, Kris Ridge or Kris Kringle. If it looks clear it's the former, that fugitive Kris Ridge may have surfaced in Blue Mountain, I'll put the word out. Until then, I'm going to need photographic evidence, partial fingerprints or a sighting by someone other than you two. And I believe that's fair."

It wasn't exactly the response they wanted.

"Okay," Hayley said after a moment.

"Thank you," Jack added.

"Give me a few minutes and I'll give you a ride back to the lodge." The chief unclipped his radio and stepped away to call for a tow truck to transport Jack's vehicle to a repair shop in town.

While watching the chief and waiting for their ride, Jack turned to Hayley. "What I want to know, is how did Ridge know exactly where and when to find us?"

She nodded. "I've been wondering the same thing."

Kris Ridge was a smart man. If he found them once, he could do it again. Or he would find Hayley, because he'd seen her clearly several times now. This fugitive had proven that he wasn't inclined to run. He would come after them until they brought Ridge in.

# TWELVE

Hayley reached for coffee while the other three bounty hunters dug into their food in the lodge suite. Once again, Milo and Katherine had fetched them a meal, and Hayley thanked them. They'd all gotten up early, and after last night's crash she desperately needed a caffeine boost. Her muscles and joints were sore and she had a pounding headache. But she was nevertheless grateful. Because things could have ended up worse. So much worse.

"Maybe there isn't just one person in town helping Ridge and getting information to him," Milo said after everyone had claimed their food and coffee and settled into place on the sofa or chairs. The question of how Ridge had known Jack and Hayley's location last night was the current topic of conversation. "Maybe there's a network of people."

"Or it could be that no one is helping him,"

Katherine said. "Maybe he was able to learn Hayley's identity soon after she recognized him and he's been tailing her ever since. So he would have known that she was at that Corner Pocket bar, that she was staying here at the lodge while she was in town and that she'd have to go home eventually. And that's when he stole the truck and came after her." She glanced at Jack. "And you were just in the wrong place at the wrong time."

"Maybe you're right," Hayley said. "But even so, I can't shake the feeling that something's going on right in front of us that we just can't see." She glanced over at Jack, who had some cuts and bruises on his face similar to her own. "We still don't know the connection between Ridge and Barry Foster."

"I've been thinking about that," Jack said. "Ridge got away with a lot of money, enough to bribe someone to help him hide for a while. But it's been fifteen years. Along with paying out the bribe cash he would have needed money to live on. Plus there's the added financial pressure that unless he keeps paying the bribe, the person or persons who know he's in town would likely turn him into the authorities for the reward money. That million-dollar reward the armored car company put up has got to be pretty enticing. Maybe Foster coming to town was connected to that."

"That's a lot of maybes, boss," Katherine said.

"Just trying to come up with some working theories," Jack said before taking a forkful of scrambled eggs.

After a few moments of silence as they ate, Katherine turned to Hayley. "I guess the good news is you're no longer the only person who's seen Ridge. Killing you won't solve his problem because Jack could still go on to convince people Ridge is in town and maybe eventually get the authorities to put forth a stronger effort to find him."

"Not necessarily." Hayley set aside her plate. "Silva still doesn't believe me. Or us." She glanced at Jack, who had likewise set his plate aside. "Not enough for him to make finding Ridge a priority. So instead of our fugitive no longer targeting me, it could be that now he'll intentionally target the two of us."

Jack gave her a lingering look. "Like it or not, we're in it together."

Her heart squeezed a little. Because *together*, with him, had taken on such an easy, right feeling. It was something she hadn't realized was missing from her life. Not until she found herself routinely annoyed and delighted by a man with character and insight and smarts. A man of faith.

"Yes, we are in this together," she affirmed, a little shocked to realize she actually meant it. Her competitive streak hadn't weakened. But after all she and Jack had been through, and especially now that they would both be in Kris Ridge's crosshairs, the capture seemed bigger than simply her trying to do her job. Maybe even bigger than the nod of approval from her brothers and the rest of the Range River Bail Bonds team.

She'd already had a conversation with Connor about the crash. As her boss, he needed to hear about it from her, so she'd checked in with him late last night and given her day's report. He'd immediately declared that he would drop everything to see her and make sure for himself that she was okay.

Fortunately, she'd been able to talk him out of the visit. But she had absolutely felt his concern and his love. And for some reason, at this very point in her life, she realized that she'd been trying to prove her worth to him on the job, that this drove her ambition, her work ethic, her desire to be the best bounty hunter around. She'd been feeling all this time that she had to somehow pay him back for the sacrifices he'd been forced to make when he'd agreed to raise her after her parents died. Yet Connor didn't need or expect that. He didn't need sacrifices from her.

*Thank You, Lord.* It was funny how often life lessons showed up when you least expected them.

Hayley cleared her throat and tried to shove aside the emotion of the moment. She was a bounty hunter with a job to do. "Maybe Ridge came after us last night because we're hitting too close to home with the visits to the motorcycle shops and the pool halls. Unless or until we get new leads from the cops, I say we keep doing that. Keep visiting places where he may hang out."

"Works for me," Jack said, setting aside his empty coffee mug. "And we might as well start showing his picture around. And identify ourselves as bounty hunters. He's obviously figured out we're after him by now, so there's no point in trying to be on the sneaky about it."

"Okay."

After the accident last night, Hayley had arranged for one of the Range River Bail Bonds employees to drive her SUV up to Blue Mountain and leave it parked at the lodge. Jack's truck would be out of commission for a while.

"I'm going to text Agnew and see if he learned anything last night," she added. "And I'll tell him about the attack in case he hasn't heard about it yet." She pulled her phone from her back pocket. The case and screen were cracked thanks to the truck rollover, but it still functioned.

"Katherine and I could visit a few places connected to Ridge's interests, as well," Milo suggested to Jack.

"All right."

"Let's head back to the motorcycle shops first." Hayley got to her feet. "We know with absolute certainty that Ridge has a connection to motorcycles. Maybe our efforts to form a relationship with the people working there might pay off and they'll be willing to share more, help us more."

Jack gave her a rueful smile. "So we'll be publicly admitting that our marriage is over. I can't help feeling that we didn't give it enough of a chance," he joked.

The idea of actually being married to Jack Colter had gone from being absurd to being… well, maybe not so bad. And realizing that terrified her.

"Does this mean we're going to pack it in and move back home to Range River?" Katherine asked.

Jack shook his head. "Not just yet. The lodge has worked as a pretty good base of operations. I want to stay here a little longer. Maybe we'll catch Ridge quickly. We need to."

So even though Hayley and Jack were no longer going to pretend to be married, they were still going to be together for most of their waking hours.

That was reassuring and unnerving at the same time. It was comforting to have such a capable bounty hunter close by her side. But keeping control of her feelings for him became more difficult the more time she spent around him.

Jack reached for Hayley's hand as they walked through the door of Freedom Motorsports. Several moments passed before he realized what he'd done and remembered that they weren't pretending to be a couple anymore. The funny thing was, Hayley didn't say a word about it. She didn't even pull her hand away from his until she needed to reach into the folder she was carrying to pull out Kris Ridge's photo.

"Welcome back! Have you picked out the motorcycles you want?" The saleswoman they'd spoken to on their prior visit smiled brightly.

"Actually, we're not here to talk to you about purchasing motorcycles," Hayley replied. "We'd like to talk to you about someone else who may have come in to buy a motorcycle or maybe have one repaired."

The woman drew her brows together. "I don't understand."

"I'm sorry, but we misrepresented ourselves when we were here before," Hayley continued, genuine regret evident in her voice. She held out the picture of Ridge. The saleswoman didn't take it. "We're actually bounty hunters and we're searching for a very dangerous man who rides a motorcycle and might have been in here."

The woman shifted her gaze to Jack and he nodded in confirmation.

"His name is Kris Ridge. Though you might know him by a different name. He escaped from the authorities fifteen years ago and we assume he's been living under an alias ever since then. You must know about the shooting just down the street from here yesterday morning. The assailant was Kris

Ridge. I know because he was trying to kill me. Knowing that, would you please consider helping us?"

The woman raised her brows and her jaw went slack.

"Why didn't you tell me the truth when you came in before?"

The woman seemed genuinely curious rather than angry.

"Some people are a little freaked out when a bounty hunter shows up at their home or business asking questions. We definitely aren't the police. Most people have never come across a bounty hunter, so they don't know what to do." She took a deep breath and blew it out. "I'm sorry that we weren't straightforward before. So what do you think? Will you share any information you have about him with us?"

The saleswoman hesitated and then finally reached for the photo that Hayley had been trying to hand to her. The paper trembled as she held it. Jack could clearly see that she was nervous. "We don't tell the fugitive where we got our information when a private citizen helps us. This isn't going to put you in danger."

She looked closely at the image, and Jack held his breath. The longer she looked at it, the more hopeful he became. Typically, if someone took more time to study a picture it was because the person in the photo looked at least somewhat familiar.

She held up a finger. "One minute." And then she walked over to the guy manning the repair counter and showed him the photo. They talked for a couple of minutes, keeping their voices low so that Jack and Hayley couldn't hear them.

"She recognizes him," Hayley said softly, excitement in her voice. "I'm sure of it."

Both employees returned. "I'm pretty sure the man in this picture has been in here," the woman said. She glanced at her coworker, who nodded in agreement.

"Do you remember the name he was using?" Hayley asked.

They glanced at each other again and shook their heads.

"Did you see what kind of vehicle he arrived in?" Jack asked. "Was he with someone else? Can you remember any detail about him?"

Neither of them could give him the answers he and Hayley were looking for.

"Do you remember if he purchased anything?" Hayley asked.

The woman thought for a moment. "I believe he did."

Jack's heart sped up. "So you'd have re-cords of purchases." He glanced around at video cameras placed at the corners of the sales floor. "And security footage."

"Not so fast." The woman held up her hand. "If you want to give me your business card, I'll pass it along to the owner and he can call you and discuss sharing our security footage if he wants to. Or if the actual police show up and ask for it with a warrant, we would defi-nitely hand it over to them."

"We're in a hurry, so can we get the contact information for the owner?" Hayley asked.

"No."

That was a bit of a setback.

"The owner values his privacy," she added.

"Okay, well, can you tell me if he's been in here recently?" Jack asked, changing direc-tions. Trying to pressure the employees into cooperating with them wasn't going to get him anywhere. "Do you see Ridge around this part of town often?" If he could estab-lish that Ridge frequented the neighborhood, maybe they could figure out another way to track him.

"It's probably been two or three months since I've seen him." This time it was the guy who answered. "He was in here asking me about options for getting heated handle grips when the weather turns cooler."

"Did he order anything?" Jack asked hopefully.

"Not that I recall."

The bounty hunters hadn't gotten the specific information which could lead to the capture that they'd hoped for, but they did have confirmation that Ridge had been seen in town by someone other than themselves. And if the motorcycle shop owner turned out to be helpful, they might get images that would convince Chief Silva to prioritize Ridge's capture. Maybe even get him to call in the feds or other local agencies that could offer manpower and resources.

Hayley pulled a couple of business cards from her satchel and handed them over. "If the owner would call me I'd appreciate it. And if either of you remember anything later— or if Ridge actually comes into your shop— give me a call."

The saleswoman looked at the card and then returned her gaze to Hayley. "If he comes back into the shop, I'm calling the police."

Hayley nodded. "That's a very good idea."

On their way out of the shop, Hayley

checked her phone and read aloud the reply Agnew had sent in response to her earlier text. "Visited a few bars. Didn't see or over-hear anything helpful. Will reach out to my informants. Heard about the wreck over the police radio. Glad you two are okay."

"I say we go by the police department and tell Silva what we've learned," Hayley said as she tucked her phone away. "He can get a warrant to view the Freedom Motorsports security footage and he can finally see Ridge for himself. Maybe he can get access to order records or something, match them up with the time Ridge was in the store, and we can finally know Kris Ridge's alias."

"Let's do it," Jack said. "We could look up the owner of Motorsports in public re-cords and contact him ourselves, but going the police route will likely be quicker and get more results." Identifying Ridge's alias and showing his picture around in town and on-line should speed things up as they tried to find him. But that could also mean that Ridge would accelerate his efforts to get at Hayley. Past history showed that Ridge did not like to concede any situation that he viewed as a competition.

Jack glanced over at Hayley, noting her

bruises and cuts as a result of last night's incident. He wouldn't refer to it as an accident when it was so clearly a murder attempt. The attacks against Hayley had been going on for too long. First Barry Foster, now Kris Ridge. Jack was ready to go full throttle on the chase for Ridge. Enough was enough.

When Jack and Hayley arrived at the chief's office, Silva was on his phone, pacing behind his desk. He waved them in as he continued talking.

"Keep trying," he said to the caller. "If we can't get anywhere within the next hour, I'll check with Judge Harrison and see if I can get a warrant to search the property." He hung up and turned to the bounty hunters. "As you can see, I'm busy this morning. You texted me that you wanted to meet, you said it was important. So, what have you got?"

"Have you made any progress on the vehicular attack last night?" Jack asked.

The chief tilted his head and gave him an exasperated look. "Is that what you're here for? I told you I'd keep you updated if we learned anything significant. So far, we haven't."

"That's not the only reason why we want to see you," Hayley quickly interjected. "We have some information that might help with the search for Kris Ridge."

"Getting traction on the investigation of last night's incident is my top priority," the chief said tightly.

There was a light rap on the open door and Agnew walked in. After a brief, general greeting, he turned his attention to Silva. "Parker told me to check in with you. Said you could use some extra help this morning."

"Yeah, I'm going to need all hands on deck today." Silva was still standing, so everyone else remained standing, as well. The message was clear that he had things to do.

"We took possession of the assailant truck from last night, but we still haven't been able to talk to the registered owner." Silva directed his comments to all three visitors in his office. "It's connected to a small company that operates on a contracted basis, so they don't have regular office hours. Since I couldn't reach the owner by phone, I sent officers to the facility this morning, but there was no one there." He gestured toward the phone that he'd just set on his desk. "My next step is to get a warrant so I can search the property and see if there's evidence of foul play, that something bad might have happened to the owner. I'm in the process of trying to obtain that warrant right now."

"So you think Ridge—or whoever was driving the truck last night—somehow disabled the owner when they stole the truck?" Hayley asked. "That they physically harmed him?"

Silva pressed his lips together in a grim line and nodded. "It's a possibility. But I don't have compelling evidence that someone is in imminent danger. So it's taking longer than I'd like, but we will make our way in there."

"Ridge is getting desperate," Jack said. "And someone like him, feeling threatened, is only going to get more dangerous."

"Right now my job is to follow the evidence wherever it leads," Silva said. "I'm still not assuming anything, but I'm not ruling anything out, either. Maybe Kris Ridge is behind the attack on you two last night. Maybe he is somehow tied to Barry Foster. If that's the case, the evidence will point us in that direction."

Parker walked up to the open office door, knocked lightly and said to the chief, "We've located the owner's sister and left her a message. Hopefully she'll return our call and help us talk to her brother."

Silva nodded and then turned back to the bounty hunters. "What is the new information about Ridge that you wanted to tell me?"

"We were just at Freedom Motorsports," Hayley began, and went on to explain what their visit had turned up and how they needed access to the security camera footage and past credit card payments for orders that might lead them to Ridge.

"A two-or three-month stretch would be a lot of footage to go through," Silva said. "And they could be misremembering." He shook his head. "I don't have the manpower to assign to that right now. But it could be worth following up on later, when things calm down."

"Jack and I both have staff back in Range River who could look over it," Hayley offered.

"You want the police department to obtain that footage and then hand it over to private citizens to review it?" Parker asked from his spot in the doorway. "Seriously?"

"I could look over it," Agnew offered.

"Not at the moment," Silva said quickly. "I have other plans for you."

"That's it?" Hayley asked, sounding dumbfounded. "We bring you helpful information and you're not going to act on it?"

"We'll get to it when we can. Right now I've got a lot going on and I can't act on every hunch you might have."

His phone rang and he reached for it. "Excuse me, I need to get back to work."

Realizing they'd been dismissed, the bounty hunters left.

They'd just stepped outside when Jack heard a noise behind him and turned to see Agnew following them out the door.

"Hey, I just want to tell you that the chief really is a good guy and a good cop, but he's not from around here and I'm not sure he realizes how much it would mean to people for Ridge to finally be captured. And I know for a fact he's telling the truth when he says the department barely has the financial resources it needs to properly police the town."

"He's got a right to set his own priorities," Hayley said, sounding disappointed.

"What are you planning to do next? I didn't learn anything useful from visiting the bars. Do you have any other ideas on places where he might like to hang out?"

"If his interests now are the same as they were in the past, which seems likely, we know Ridge enjoys great steaks, upscale restaurants and that he fancies himself a gourmet cook.

Milo and Katherine are checking with businesses and social groups connected to that."

Agnew smiled slightly. "I don't have anything to offer on any of that. I eat at restaurants or I microwave frozen dinners at home. I don't cook since it's just me. But I will keep trying to connect with the informants I have. If there's information about Ridge floating around, one of them will know it. They just might be a little hesitant to talk because Ridge has a reputation as a stone-cold killer. Selling him out for reward money could seem like too dangerous a risk."

After telling him that he would be in touch, Agnew went back inside.

"I keep wondering about Barry Foster's connection to Ridge." Hayley shook her head. "That mystery *really* bugs me."

Jack considered her words. Looking deeper into finding the connection between the two fugitives could be what ultimately helped them find Ridge. What they needed to do right now was take a step back, look at the big picture and consciously consider possibilities they might have been blinded to earlier.

# THIRTEEN

"You and I both know it was Ridge who attacked us last night." Hayley stood with her hands on her hips. "The truck he used was stolen in this part of town from Reliable Haul and Storage. He had to have driven here or had someone drop him here to steal it *somehow*. It's worth looking around at the adjoining streets for an abandoned vehicle."

They were one street over from Reliable Haul and Storage, in a light industrial section of Blue Mountain where there was a scattering of warehouses, stores, storefront offices and a couple of coffee stands.

"But how would we know what to look for?" Jack asked. "The only thing we've ever seen him drive other than the truck is a motorcycle." He glanced up and down the street. "And I don't see one parked around here."

"I'm still thinking about that."

An hour ago Agnew had texted Jack to let him know that Silva had spoken with the owner of the assailant truck, at last. The weaponized vehicle had in fact been stolen and the owner was more than willing to let the police have a look around.

Images of the truck thief had been caught on one of the security cameras as he'd walked across the company's parking lot, but no clear picture of his face had been captured. Since the thief didn't break into the business's office, the alarm had not been triggered. Hayley and Jack arrived at the scene only to be given those bare bones facts from Agnew and then directed to leave the property by Silva as soon as he saw them there.

Silva had every right to secure his crime scene. Hayley realized that. But she and Jack had every right to be in the surrounding neighborhood, which was where they were now.

Hayley decided how she wanted to proceed. She slid her phone out of her pocket, walked up to the nearest car, walked around it while looking in the windows and then took a picture of the license plate. "We could get lucky and see a crowbar or rope or duct tape or anything else commonly used by thieves left behind in the front seat of the car and that could indicate Ridge had driven it," she said in answer to Jack's question a few moments ago. "Whether we see those things or not, I think it's likely he stole a vehicle, drove it here and then abandoned it. He created a meticulous plan to rob the armored truck he and his coworkers were driving. We know he plans ahead."

"So we log the cars around here, see if any of them have been reported as stolen, and if so, we consider that they could have been stolen by Ridge." Jack nodded appreciatively. "Smart."

Hayley turned and snapped a picture of him. "Yeah," she said, "I know."

"All right, Ms. Smart, tell me how you think having that information would be helpful to us."

She smiled at him. "First thing, we'd check for his prints. Beyond that, we go back to the neighborhood where it was stolen from and look around. Check for security video. Show Ridge's picture around. Maybe it's near where he lives or works."

"Basic bounty hunting," Jack said. "Not always so glamorous."

"But it works. And collecting stolen vehicle reports from the police department website or the local newspaper is easy enough."

They split up and took opposite sides of the street, continuing to work until they'd covered four blocks on each of the four streets surrounding Reliable Haul and Storage.

"I'm going to call Katherine," Jack said after he and Hayley finished. "See if it's a good time for her and Milo to meet us for a late lunch and to compare notes."

"Sounds good."

They were almost to Hayley's SUV when a patrol car pulled up alongside them. Parker was at the wheel and Agnew sat in the passenger seat.

"Have you learned anything new about the truck theft?" Hayley asked Parker through his rolled-down window, hoping they'd gotten a photo or fingerprint left behind by Ridge.

"Actually, I'm following up on a 9-1-1 call." He smiled faintly and shook his head. "Somebody reported a pair of car prowlers. Looks like they meant you two."

"Not the first time I've been mistaken for a criminal while on the job." Hayley exchanged glances with Jack. "Probably won't be the last."

"So what are you two doing out here?" Parker asked.

"The first thing we did was go into a few

businesses, show Ridge's picture around and ask if anyone had seen him. When that didn't pay off, we started looking around to see if maybe he'd stolen a vehicle to get here and then left it behind."

"So you thought you'd do the police department's job?" The smile was gone from the patrolman's face now. "Didn't Silva warn you away from investigating this crime?"

"Not trying to step on your toes," Jack said easily. "Just trying to catch a bail jumper."

"Well, you *are* stepping on our toes. You're putting yourself into the middle of an active police investigation and that needs to stop." He paused for a moment, and when he spoke again he didn't sound as hostile. "You need to find some other way to track down Ridge. You're too close to crossing the line into taking police action."

Silva summoned Parker over the radio, asking him to return to the Reliable Haul and Storage building. As Parker replied, Agnew got out of the car and walked over to Hayley and Jack.

"I've got to go," Parker said through the window to Agnew. "Are you staying here with them or are you going with me?"

Agnew tilted his head toward Hayley and

Jack. "I'm going to talk to them for a minute, then I'll meet you back over at the crime scene."

"Copy that." Parker made a U-turn and drove away.

"You realize you could be putting yourself in danger by walking around out here in plain view, right?" Agnew said to Hayley.

"I realize Ridge wants me dead," Hayley said, wishing she felt as self-assured as she sounded. "All the more reason I want to do everything I can to find him and lock him up."

"I can respect that," Agnew said. "And I meant what I said earlier about questioning my informants. I know some guys who've made their living establishing false identities for other people. Everything from ID cards to completely fabricated online histories. Ridge might have interacted with them. Do you have an extra one of those printed age-enhanced photos you could give me? Might make things easier if I could show it around. Might be a little easier for some people to see than a small picture on a phone screen."

Hayley grabbed a photo from the folder in her SUV and gave it to him.

"Thanks," he said. "I'll let you know if I learn anything."

"Can I give you a ride back over to the Haul and Storage?"

He shook his head. "It's just a block away, I can walk. And if everybody's left the scene when I get there, I'll call Parker to come back and pick me up. He'll love that." Agnew grinned,

"What do you know about Parker?" Jack asked.

Agnew shrugged. "Same things everybody else knows, I suppose. He came up here from Boise about the time Silva showed up, although he says they didn't know each other beforehand. I put in a fair number of hours as a reserve officer, a lot of them with Parker. My kids are grown, my wife passed away after a long illness and I'm not one to just sit around the house. He's not a bad guy. He was pretty friendly and easygoing at first, but then he changed. Became a little more edgy, like he is now. I have no idea why. Could be it's just his personality or the job's worn him down."

With that, Agnew turned and started walking in the direction of the haul and storage company.

Hayley watched him go, thinking about what he'd said. About the change in Parker after he'd been in Blue Mountain for a while, and about the possibility that Hayley's willingness to get out and look for Ridge made it easier for him to target and try to kill her.

"At least it's not raining this time," Hayley said as Jack opened the door on their second visit to Corner Pocket and they stepped into the neon illumination of the bar.

After meeting with Katherine and Milo for pizza and the chance for both teams to recap what they'd learned so far—which was nothing useful, really—the couple had parted ways again. Katherine and Milo had resumed visiting businesses related to Ridge's food interests since dining tastes were something people rarely changed. Hayley and Jack had invested time in looking at the social media accounts for the establishments in town with an active pool-shooting draw, but they didn't see anyone who looked like Ridge.

Now that it was early evening they were returning to the bars they'd previously visited, this time showing Kris Ridge's picture to employees and pool-shooting patrons and asking if anyone recognized him. Corner Pocket, the place they felt was most likely to appeal to Ridge, was their first stop.

Hayley moved forward toward the cluster

of people at the bar with Jack by her side, conscious that he did not casually drape his arm over her shoulders like he had the last time they were here. Pretending to be husband and wife.

She didn't want to admit to herself that she missed that. Missed the feeling of her and Jack being a couple, holding hands, sticking together and looking out for one another.

But she did miss it.

She headed toward Mischa, a bartender she and Jack had befriended on their prior visit, once again hoping that their investment of nonthreatening friendliness ahead of time would pay off. At this point, the fugitive obviously knew at least two bounty hunters were actively pursuing him. The opportunity to take him by surprise and grab him without warning had passed.

After waiting for a break in the flow of drink orders, Hayley stepped up and offered Mischa a friendly greeting. Once she'd ordered a cola for herself and one for Jack, and added a sizable tip to her payment, Hayley leaned forward and said, "Hey, can I ask you something?"

"Of course." Mischa set her elbows on the bar and leaned slightly forward so she could hear better.

Hayley pulled out a photo of Ridge and set it on the bar. "Have you ever seen this man?"

Mischa peered at the picture. "That looks like Gavin Shaw."

Hayley's heart sped up. *A name.* They finally had a potential alias for Ridge! Her hands trembled slightly with the surge of adrenaline as she quickly texted the name to Maribel and asked her to research it as soon as possible. Only then did she exchange a glance with Jack. The smile on his lips was slight, but the intensity in his gaze showed that he was as excited as she was to finally get this lead.

Mischa waved over a server loading up her tray with drinks, and the woman leaned forward to get a look at the photo. "Oh, yeah, Gavin," she said with a smile. "He's in here fairly often. Nice guy. Why are you asking about him?"

*Nice guy?* Hayley sighed. That was one of the scariest things about the criminals she chased. Many of them were master manipulators. And they were good at getting people to trust them.

"Actually, my husb-, my *partner* and I are bounty hunters." How had she gotten so used to referring to Jack as her husband in such a short amount of time? She shook her head slightly and refocused her thoughts. "This man is Kris Ridge," Hayley said, tapping the photo. "He murdered two people in cold blood in the course of an armored car robbery and he's been a fugitive for fifteen years."

Mischa, who'd been studying the photo, looked up at Hayley and Jack with her jaw dropped.

The server resumed studying the picture and nodded to herself saying, "Yeah, I'm sure that's Gavin." She looked up at Hayley. "And you're saying he's a murderer and a fugitive?"

Someone called out impatiently to the server for their drinks. She waved them off without even looking at them and kept her attention riveted on Hayley and Jack. "And you two are bounty hunters?" she asked, her eyes practically glittering with fascination.

Hayley's mind raced with questions she wanted to ask the two women. Like whether they'd heard Ridge—or Shaw, as they knew him—ever mention where in town he lived, or where he worked, or a business he owned. Maybe where he kept a boat. Anything that might include a detail that would help them find him.

She took a steadying breath, because she would gain nothing if she overwhelmed them.

"Do you remember what kind of vehicle he drives?" she managed to ask calmly. This was north Idaho. He would need to have a car or truck, something other than the motorcycle to get around in the depth of winter.

The server opened her mouth to speak just as a patron walked up, flashed her a disgruntled look and then grabbed two drinks off her serving tray, which was still sitting on the bar. He stomped back to his table.

The cocktail server rolled her eyes at the customer's impatience and then said, "I've seen Gavin get into a black sedan. Kind of sporty looking. Give me a minute and I'll think of what kind it was."

Before she could recall, a man wearing several flashy gold rings stepped up beside her. "People want their drinks, Nikki, what's the holdup?" He spotted the photo still laying on the bar and then turned to the bounty hunters. "What's going on?"

"Have you seen this man?" Jack asked.

"I might have seen him come in a few times. Likes to play in the pool tournaments. Why? Who's asking? Are you two cops?"

"Bounty hunters," Hayley answered, turning on her friendliest smile. "And you are?" They were *finally* getting some traction on

Kris Ridge. They had a name, a general vehicle description and they'd obviously found a bar he liked to frequent. Just a little more information and they could quickly be on their way to grabbing him.

"I own this place," the man said. "And I'm not interested in ratting out a paying customer to a couple of bounty hunters."

Mischa and Nikki quickly tried to explain to him who Kris Ridge was and about the violent things he'd done, but the bar owner wanted no part of it. "I sell drinks," he said to the bounty hunters. "I create an atmosphere where people want to hang out and have a good time. As far as I'm concerned, it's my job to protect my customers' anonymity. We're not talking to anybody but actual cops." He turned to his employees. "Let's get back to work."

Hayley finished her cola, and as the owner turned to speak with another server, she subtly passed her business card to Mischa. "Thank you."

The bartender nodded and slipped the card into her pocket. Hayley hoped that was an indication that she intended to call her later and answer the rest of her questions.

Since Hayley and Jack were obviously no longer welcome there, they headed for the exit.

Hayley checked her phone while they were on the narrow walkway outside. "I've got a text from Maribel. She got some hits for Gavin Shaw in Idaho but nothing specifically in Blue Mountain. She's going to keep digging."

"I missed a call from Agnew while we were in there," Jack said as soon as she finished speaking. He held his phone up to his ear to listen to the message. "He says he's got something to talk to us about." Jack tapped the screen to return the call and then set it on speaker.

Agnew picked up the call and once they got their greetings out of the way Jack asked, "Have you ever heard the name Gavin Shaw?"

There was a brief pause on the other end before Agnew said, "That name's not ringing any bells."

"We just got a lead that it might be the name Ridge is currently using. Or at least one of the names."

"I'm in my personal vehicle right now," Agnew said. "As soon as I get off the phone with you I'll call Silva and he can run it through the departmental database."

"Good," Jack said. "Meanwhile, I am returning your call. Did you have anything for us?"

"I checked with some of the informants I've cultivated over the years. One of the older guys who used to make fake IDs said Ridge paid him twenty times his normal fee for an extensive false background with a driver's license, credit cards, the works. But Ridge also said he'd kill the guy's entire family if he ever gave him up to the cops."

"So why would he be willing to help us capture him now?"

"He's recently sober after a lot of years of drugs and drinking and he's trying to make amends. Plus I suggested that you might be willing to kick a little of your bounty recovery fee money in his direction if he helped you out."

"I see," Jack said with a glance at Hayley, who nodded her head in response.

"What's the next step?" Jack asked.

"The informant's name is Broady and I'm on my way to his house to talk to him now. He says he's not willing to talk to me over any kind of electronic device—it has to be face-to-face. Otherwise, he's afraid the conversation will be recorded and somehow it will get back to Ridge that Broady informed on him. That's also why I'm driving over in my own truck to talk to him instead of taking a patrol car. I'm doing everything I can to keep him calm so he doesn't change his mind and clam up."

"Makes sense," Jack said.

"If one or both of you want to come along, great. If not, I'll report back to you."

"I want to go," Hayley said to Jack.

"All right," Jack said toward the phone. "We're in. What's the address?"

"It's off Shale Road on the west side of the lake. It's kind of hard to find. It would be easier if you rode with me or followed me. Where are you right now?"

"Corner Pocket."

"Okay, I'm not far from there. Be there in a minute."

They ended the call and a few minutes later Agnew pulled into Corner Pocket's small parking lot.

"Did you remember to call Silva after you talked to us and give him the Gavin Shaw alias to check on?" Hayley asked as soon as he pulled to a stop.

She was hoping for an arrest tonight. Once they talked to Agnew's informant and the police ran Ridge's alias—or aliases—they should be able to use the connected vehicle registration, credit card transactions and cell phone information to track him.

"I'll call Silva on the way to the informant's house," Agnew told Hayley.

The bounty hunters got into Hayley's SUV. Before they drove off behind Agnew, she sent a quick text to Silva. Just in case the former chief forgot to call him.

The drive took them to the lake, then westward around its perimeter as Agnew had said it would. The chief turned off onto a road with widely spaced houses and stretches of forest between them. Hayley had to agree that in the dark, even with GPS, it would have been tricky to find the location.

Finally, Agnew made a turn onto a long unpaved drive. He followed it to a house, where he pulled off to the side and parked in the grass. Hayley pulled off to park behind him.

She smiled at Jack as they walked up to Agnew, excited to put some life into the chase, to get moving and finally slap handcuffs on Kris Ridge. It occurred to her that at this point she couldn't care less who got credit for the capture. Range River Bail Bonds, Eagle River Bail Bonds, the Blue Mountain Police Department. It didn't matter. For the sake of justice and the victims' families, she just wanted to see Ridge captured and locked up.

The house in front of them was pleasant looking, with a wide porch holding a trio of rocking chairs and a couple of large ceramic pots with small evergreen trees growing out of them.

Agnew walked up the steps, stopped in front of the door and then put his phone to his ear. "Yeah, Broady. It's me and the friends I told you about."

Hayley and Jack walked up behind him and waited.

The bolt in the door's lock made a loud clicking sound as it slid out of place.

The door opened.

"Broady," Agnew said, stepping aside.

Hayley saw the shadowed figure of a man outlined by the light shining from the room behind him. He took a step forward, turned slightly. A moment too late she saw that he held a gun.

He pointed it at the bounty hunters and fired.

# FOURTEEN

"Gun!" Jack leaped on Hayley as the man started shooting, covering her body with his as they rolled across the porch and dropped onto the ground.

All the while, Jack heard more gunfire, and realized the shooter was moving toward them.

He got to his feet and reached for Hayley's hand. Illumination from the lights shining out of the house windows made them easy targets.

Hayley was already grabbing for her weapon. He knew the feeling; he wanted to fight back, too. But first they needed the cover of darkness. "Head for the trees!" Broady's house was surrounded by forest. It was their best chance to get out of the range of Broady's gunshots.

"What about Agnew?" Hayley looked toward the house. "We can't just leave him!"

"He probably jumped off the other end of the porch and got away. Come on, let's *go!*"

She hesitated a moment longer, and then snapped a quick nod before turning and racing across the narrow strip of lawn toward the tree line. Jack ran with her, bullets kicking up the turf around them and splintering the trunks of the trees just ahead of them.

As they finally entered the forest, rocky, uneven ground slowed their pace. Vines and bushes sprouting from patches of dirt and covering chunks of rock seemed to grab at Jack's ankles and try to trip him. Fortunately, Hayley was lighter on her feet and able to move faster. It made for one less thing for him to worry about. Hayley was perfectly competent—more than competent—but Jack couldn't keep himself from wanting to watch out for her.

Broady fired the whole time they ran, even after they entered the deeper darkness of the forest.

Jack's mind raced with thoughts of a plan to stay alive while also helping the former police chief. He hoped Agnew had also escaped into the forest, but he might have been too injured to make it that far. Or worse, he could be lying wounded somewhere. Or dead. He consoled himself with the thought that Broady seemed intent on getting Hayley and him, and not Agnew, so running might at least keep the shooter away from the former police chief.

Jack considered the terrifying possibility that the shooter had night vision equipment. He and Hayley would know soon enough. If Broady followed them into the darkness and his shots were accurate, that meant he had night vision and they'd have to hunker down and hide until help arrived. Or until Broady ran out of bullets. And Agnew would be on his own.

Finally, the shooting stopped.

Hayley stopped running and turned back to Jack. He caught up with her and they both dropped down, each of them gasping and working to catch their breath. By that point both of them had drawn their weapons.

Jack tried to breathe as quietly as he could while listening for any sound that Broady had followed them into the forest. Hayley, who alternated her attention between the direction of the house they'd just run from and the woods surrounding them, was apparently doing the same thing.

"What just happened?" Hayley whispered.

Jack knew exactly what she meant. It had seemed like the meeting with Agnew's informant would go fine. According to the retired chief, Broady had agreed to talk.

"Do you think Ridge got to him?" Hayley asked. "He knew that Broady was aware of his true identity. Maybe he renewed his threat to kill Broady's family since Ridge knows we're in town tracking him."

"No telling." Jack reached for his phone to call for help. "Agnew said Broady had a history of addiction problems. Maybe he relapsed into that. He could have some sort of residual paranoia as a result of it." Shielding the screen with his hand so it wouldn't give away their position in the darkness, he tapped in 9-1-1. At the same time, he noticed a single bar of connectivity that flickered on and off. "I can't get a stable connection." With the volume turned down to its bare minimum, he held the phone to his ear. He didn't hear ringing. He didn't even hear static.

He looked at Hayley and shook his head. The property they were on was in a drainage channel formed by the runoff of water down the mountainside. Jack glanced up at the nearby ridge at the side of what was basically a narrow canyon. Maybe they could get phone reception if they climbed up there. But that would be a long hike. And it could be possible that Agnew needed medical help right away.

"Maybe we need to get back closer to the road," Hayley said.

She could be right. Cell coverage in the mountains of north Idaho often didn't conform to a logical pattern and a small move could make a big difference in connectivity.

They took a few moments to listen for sounds that Broady was coming after them, but they didn't hear anything. They began moving as stealthily as they could through the forest, heading back in the direction of Broady's house and the road.

When they reached the edge of Broady's lawn, Jack spotted Hayley's SUV. It was still sitting in the same place where she'd parked it. Maybe they should just run for that and try to get in and drive away.

The front door of the house was closed. The front porchlight was out.

"Maybe Broady left or went inside and passed out or something," Hayley whispered.

"Or maybe he's waiting inside your SUV figuring we'll take the bait for an easy escape." Jack was pondering their options when he heard a voice. After a moment, he realized it was Virgil Agnew. And he was apparently behind the house. He might desperately need their help.

The former chief stopped talking.

Jack motioned to Hayley he was going to have a look and that she should stay put.

She elbowed him aside and moved forward. They proceeded together for a few steps, paused and then Agnew's voice became audible again. "Broady, listen to me. It's going to be okay," he called out.

Classic example of the tone of voice cops used when they wanted to calm down an agitated person. "Whatever Ridge is paying you, whatever threat he's holding over you, it's not worth it for you to do this. Killing me will only mean a life sentence for you. You'll never get away with it."

"Broady's about to kill him!" Hayley whispered.

Tension and fear fired the nerves across Jack's entire body. They couldn't just leave the scene. They couldn't wait until they got a phone connection and were able to call the police. They had to do something to save Agnew *now.*

"Get ready to head around the corner of the house," Hayley said. "You aim high, I'll aim low. If we can, let's tackle Broady to the ground. I don't want to fire unless we have to."

"Agreed," Jack said.

"No!" Agnew screamed, the sound drowned by subsequent rapid gunfire.

Jack and Hayley sprinted around the corner of the house and then pulled up short.

Former chief Agnew and a familiar-looking figure stood side by side on the back porch in a half circle of light shining from a fixture attached to the house. Agnew looked perfectly fine. He and the man beside him both pointed their guns at the bounty hunters.

Shock seemed to freeze Jack's thoughts for a moment as he struggled to understand what he was seeing.

"Looks like your chase is over," Agnew said. He gestured at the man beside him. "Meet my informant Broady."

"Also known as Gavin Shaw," the familiar-looking man said. "Back in the old days, they used to call me Kris Ridge. Now, drop your weapons."

The bounty hunters had entered the trap before they'd had time to adjust the aim of their guns. Their weapons were not precisely directed at the bad guys. Ridge and Agnew, on the other hand, had their pistols pointed directly at *them*. If the bounty hunters did anything other than obey the order, they would both be shot in the head in an instant.

They dropped their guns.

"What?" Hayley was barely able to get even that single word out of her mouth. The gut punch of surprise at seeing Blue Mountain's former police chief and Kris Ridge working together made it hard for her to draw the breath she needed to speak.

"Don't blame Agnew here," Kris Ridge said. "I was the one who figured you'd probably come running if you thought he was in trouble."

Hayley turned to the former police chief, who lifted his chin with an expression that managed to look both ashamed and defiant at the same time. "You helped Kris Ridge hide all this time?" she asked. "After he murdered his coworkers in cold blood? *Why?*"

"Everybody's got their price," Ridge interjected, sounding proud of the observation.

Hayley's mind raced back to the investigative work Maribel had done. She'd reported that Agnew didn't own an elaborate home. Hayley had already noticed that his clothes weren't particularly high quality, and his truck was midpriced and looked at least eight years old.

"Evelyn," Agnew finally said.

He'd mentioned his wife had passed away after a lengthy illness, but Hayley didn't remember him ever mentioning her name. "Your wife?"

He nodded.

"Even with insurance, health care is expensive," Ridge said. "So is hiring a home health aide to hang around the house so the poor person who's suffering isn't left alone."

An expression of pain briefly crossed Agnew's face and then it was gone.

"It took me a little while to find someone who could help me out and who also needed *my* help," Ridge said with a self-satisfied smile. "But I did."

Hayley knew why Ridge was bothering to explain himself before he killed them. It was a chance to gloat over his cleverness. He'd managed to get something over on somebody, yet again.

"How does Barry Foster tie into all of this?" Jack asked.

It was a good question. Plus keeping Agnew and Ridge talking might help put them off their guard. Even if one or both of them were only slightly distracted, that might be enough to give the bounty hunters the edge to do something. Like reach down and retrieve their guns from the ground where they'd dropped them.

"Foster's an idiot," Ridge said. "He wasn't smart enough to plan what he was doing. Thinking he could just show up in Blue Mountain and start his own drug distribution network. Didn't even consider that he could have competition."

Hayley heard a car pulling up in front of the house before Ridge could elaborate any further. A car door opened, and then what sounded like voices on a radio carried to them. Agnew and Ridge moved around until they were behind Jack and Hayley, still able to keep their guns pointed at them without being obvious, still in complete control.

Forced to listen quietly, Hayley heard someone climb the steps to the front porch and then knock on the door. A few moments later, she heard footsteps going back down the steps.

*Please don't leave.*

There was the sound of footfalls around the end of the house, and then a familiar voice called out, "Hello?"

Officer Parker appeared around the end of the building.

Hayley hoped the strange positioning of the four people standing on the patio would trigger some kind of helpful response from the newly arriving officer. But his reaction to what he saw was disappointing. "Looks like something interesting is going on," he said.

"Ridge has money," Agnew called out to Parker. "Enough money for us all. We just need to work with him."

The patrolman pursed his lips together and nodded, his gaze lingering on Ridge. "Is that right?"

Hayley's heart sank. It looked like Parker was a dirty cop, too. He was not going to help them. She and Jack had to help themselves.

Bracing herself for the impact of a bullet if the worse thing happened, Hayley took advantage of the distraction and dove for her gun.

Jack did the same thing.

Someone shot first—Hayley didn't see who it was—and in an instant everyone was shooting. A bullet struck the light fixture, plunging the expanse of backyard into darkness.

Hayley and Jack ducked and scrambled to get away from the melee. At one point Jack gasped and stumbled. Hayley doubled back and reached for his hand. He tried to wave her onward. "Go!"

"No!" she shouted back, determined that he hear her above the surrounding sounds of gunfire. How could he possibly think that she'd keep going without him? After so much intense work time together, he had to know how much she cared about him.

Didn't he?

How could he not? During the course of their pretend marriage they'd become partners. *True* partners.

She grabbed his arm as he pushed himself to his feet and they took off running again. Only he wasn't moving as quickly this time. Did he twist his ankle? Was he shot?

Determined to protect him, Hayley kept hold of him and continued running. It felt like it took forever to get past the edge of the lawn and back into the forest again. Only this time, they'd gone in the opposite direction from where they'd been before. They could run through this section of forest and eventually intersect with the road. While it looked like they were in the middle of nowhere, Ridge's house was situated in a small community.

Encouraged by the prospect of getting to a neighbor's house, or maybe even getting a phone connection once they were on the road, Hayley kept pushing on.

And Jack kept lagging behind. His breathing getting more ragged.

Hayley didn't feel like they'd gone nearly far enough to be safe, but she could tell Jack was having trouble so she stopped where they could hide behind a downed tree. So far, she had no indication Ridge or either of the two lawmen had followed them, so maybe they'd be safe enough while Jack rested for a moment.

Both of them slid down to the ground in the darkness. Hayley reached out to give Jack a reassuring pat on his leg in the darkness.

But instead of the sensation of touching denim, as she'd expected, she felt her hand covered in something damp and thick and at the same time she detected a coppery smell.

*No.*

Cupping her hand around her phone to keep from giving their position away, she turned on her flashlight app and saw blood on Jack's leg. Lots of it, from his thigh down to his calf. "You've been shot," she said, instantly flicking off the flashlight and tucking it away so she could tear off the bottom hem of her shirt and make a bandage.

Jack laughed weakly at her efforts. "I appreciate your energy, kid, but we don't have time for this."

*"Kid?"* She feigned outrage as her heart threatened to break.

"Hayley!" Agnew's voice made her jump. It was accompanied by the sound of clumsy steps in the forest, with twigs and branches snapping. The former chief was looking for them and he wasn't even trying to be subtle. "Hayley!" he called out again. "I saw the blood trail. I saw Jack get hit. It's bad, and you're scared. I don't blame you." More twigs snapped as he moved closer. "Let's talk. We can work out something. There's plenty of Ridge's money for everybody, and Jack needs medical attention. Come on, talk to me. We'll make a deal. We'll get him the help he needs."

"No," Jack whispered softly enough for only Hayley to hear.

"Of course not," she whispered back.

She was close enough to feel him shiver. The temperature had dropped, and if any precipitation fell overnight it would come down as snow. She moved closer to Jack, hoping to help keep him warm. He'd lost a lot of blood, which meant he could be in danger of going into shock. Or worse.

After a few moments of silence, it seemed certain Agnew had walked away.

Hayley turned to Jack, his face only inches

from hers. He reached over to brush her hair from her eyes, and tuck it behind her ear. He tracked his fingertip down the side of her cheek to her chin. She must have made the decision to lean toward him, though she wasn't conscious of it, and then they were kissing.

As his lips pressed against hers and their breaths mingled, the sensation was not at all what she would have imagined. His touch was gentle and loving and warm. There was no sense of him being older, or a competitor, or that she was somehow betraying her family and their business by giving in to this feeling of being drawn toward him.

Pretending to be married while they were undercover seemed to have closed the monumental gap that had previously existed between them. And she liked the feeling of being this close to him. She liked it *a lot*.

After a moment, the kiss ended. Though she didn't really want it to. She realized her hand was on his shoulder and she let it linger there.

"I have an idea," Jack whispered as she started to get up.

Hayley let her hand fall away, and immediately missed that physical connection between them. "What is it?"

"I'm going to head back to the house."

*"What?"*

"I'm going to head back to the house," he repeated calmly. "I'll draw some attention to the backyard while you're in the front, jumping into your SUV and going to get help."

"No," she said firmly. "You'll be putting yourself in danger. I won't let you do it."

He flashed her his familiar, cocky grin. "I don't remember asking your permission."

They were both standing now and she looked into his eyes, shaking her head. "It's too great a risk for you." Her heart broke as she wondered if he'd kissed her because he knew this was the end. No. She wouldn't let it be the end. "You can't move that quickly and—"

"I thought finding you would be more of a challenge." The interrupting voice belonged to Kris Ridge, who'd managed to sneak up on them. He was twenty feet away, a gun in his hand and an arrogant smile on his face. "It might be fun to let the chase go on a little longer, but I really need to wrap things up."

"Get to your SUV," Jack said, giving Hayley a sudden push that made her stumble. Though it clearly wasn't Jack's intention, she took advantage of the opportunity and lunged at Ridge. She wouldn't let this be the end for Jack or for her, or them together.

Startled by the sudden movement, Ridge pointed his gun to fire at Jack.

But Hayley raised her weapon now, too, her gaze and aim steady, her heart and mind filled with the strong conviction that she could do this, she could protect Jack, the man she cared about more deeply than she'd been willing to admit.

She fired first, hitting Ridge twice in the upper arm. He jerked halfway around and dropped his gun. Hayley was on him in an instant, knocking him to the ground and cuffing him.

"You got him," Jack said, sounding happy but also like he was losing strength.

Hayley needed to get him to a hospital. Ridge, too, although both shots had struck the fleshy part of his arm and not gone near any vital organs.

"Hayley! Jack!" The voice of Officer Parker called out to them in the forest and Hayley wasn't sure what to do. Was he a good guy, would he help the bounty hunters? Or was he on the side of Ridge and the corrupt former police chief?

Ridge's cursing and groaning as he lay on the ground gave them no indication.

Hayley turned to Jack, who appeared unsteady on his feet. She moved toward him, away from Ridge. If the captured fugitive somehow managed to get away, she would find him again. Right now all she cared about was Jack. And keeping him safe. If Parker had come looking for them with the same intent as Ridge, to kill them, she would fight him with every ounce of her being to keep Jack and herself safe.

She heard steps in the darkness. More than one person. It had to be Parker and Agnew together. She readied herself to fight both of them while Jack did his best to hold his ground beside her.

Parker called out their names again. And then, a few moments later, he stepped through the trees. Agnew was beside him, hands cuffed behind his back.

At the same time, Hayley heard emergency sirens.

"You got him," Parker said, glancing down at Ridge.

"And you called for backup?" Hayley asked hesitantly, still uncertain if she could trust him.

"I did. As soon as the shooting started behind the house. I figured you two were going to stir up something the minute you hit town. I just didn't know what it was going to be." He peered at Jack. "You all right?"

"I've been better."

Parker keyed his collar mic. "Two in custody. Kris Ridge and Virgil Agnew."

"What?" Chief Silva's voice came through the radio.

"Confirm Ridge and Agnew," Parker said. "And roll EMS for two people with gunshot wounds."

Hayley heard more radio chatter beyond that, but she wasn't listening to it. She turned to Jack, stepping toward him until he slipped his arms around her waist and pulled her close. "We did it," she said. "We captured Kris Ridge."

"*You* did it." He leaned down and pressed his forehead against hers. She noticed that he felt a little feverish. "This capture is *yours*," he said. "I'll get the next one."

*The next one.* There wasn't likely to be a *next one*. It wasn't at all likely that they would pursue another fugitive together. Combining the two rival agencies for what turned out to be two manhunts was a one-off kind of thing. It hadn't happened before and she couldn't imagine it happening again.

Their pretend marriage had somehow turned into a real connection. One with depth. In her mind, at least. She shouldn't have let it happen, but she hadn't been able to help herself. She'd started out thinking that Jack Colter was an arrogant jerk with no consideration for the rules of bounty hunting. And she'd been wrong.

She lingered in his embrace, not wanting to let go. Because she knew what came next. This hunt was over. The emotional intensity of the capture team working together would fade. The kiss they'd shared was not any kind of promise for the future. It was simply the emotion of the moment. Deep emotion for her, but who knew what it really meant to him?

Maybe she would cross paths with Jack in the future. Maybe not.

Cop cars rolled up to Ridge's house. Jack was adamant he could make the short hike back in that direction. Ridge was also able to walk. The ambulances would be arriving soon.

Trying to ignore the empty ache in her heart and the sense of loneliness already rushing in to fill it, Hayley gave Jack one more squeeze with her arms wrapped around him. And then she let him go.

# FIFTEEN

"You're still here." Jack smiled when he saw Hayley late the next morning as he limped from his bedroom into the shared living room suite at Bear's Lair Lodge.

Milo and Katherine were still there, as well, sitting with Hayley and sipping coffee.

Hayley and Jack had been out late the night before giving Chief Silva their statements regarding the night's events. After that, they'd gone to the hospital to get treatment the paramedic had suggested for him. The gunshot that wounded his leg had not left behind any fragments so he didn't need surgery. The gauze and bandages the paramedic had used to control the bleeding were replaced with a few stitches and he'd been given approval to leave as long as he promised to be careful.

Hayley had stayed by his side the whole time. She hadn't abandoned him when things got tough. Or tedious. He hadn't really needed confirmation that she had depth of character. That, despite her relative youth, she wasn't just a kid. But he'd been given that confirmation, nevertheless. The result was comforting and terrifying at the same time. Because he'd been forced to admit that he no longer had an excuse not to let himself fall in love with her.

Of course, he already had fallen in love with her.

Whether she had the same depth of feeling, or whether their shared kiss was simply the high emotion of the moment, still remained to be seen.

But despite his fear, he allowed himself to hope.

Moving slowly, because his leg was stiff and sore, he eased himself down onto the sofa beside her. "I figured you would have woken up and gone back home by now."

She shrugged. "I wasn't in a hurry."

"And it looks like you aren't, either," Milo teased his boss. "It's nearly nine o'clock. You'd normally have at least a couple of hours' work in by now." He grinned. "You're slowing down in your old age."

Jack laughed. Because he could. Normally, being the first one up, the first one to start working, the first one to complete a job, was important to him. *Proving* his worth was important to him. But now, well, now the reality that his worth wasn't measured by what he did was finally sinking in. Opening his heart to Hayley had opened up a whole different perspective on love and value, forgiveness and grace. Especially grace. Because the renewed ability to love was an example of grace, of something he hadn't *earned*. But now he realized he could accept it. Even if the potential for a broken heart was still there.

Katherine brought him a cup of coffee and he took a couple of sips.

"How are you feeling?" Hayley asked. "Triumphant? Accomplished? *Heroic?*" She grinned at him.

"Happy." And peaceful. For the first time in a very long time.

He tried not to stare, but he felt compelled to drink in the sight of her. He would miss seeing her face every morning. Their pretend marriage, short-lived as it was, might have ruined him for greeting the day completely alone. Or simply for starting any day without her.

Katherine's phone chimed and a moment later there was a knock on the door. "That would be Chief Silva," she said.

"That's right," Hayley piped up. "Apparently he called your phone but you were enjoying your beauty sleep too much to answer. So he called Katherine and said he wanted to come by before we left town."

Milo opened the door and Silva walked in accompanied by Parker.

The lawmen politely refused offers of coffee.

"We won't be long," Silva said. "I just wanted to come by and extend my appreciation for what you've done for the town of Blue Mountain. And to let you know that, at Hayley's request, both of your agencies are listed as having recovered Ridge. So the bounty payment will be an equal fifty-fifty split."

Jack turned to Hayley and she smiled at him. It confirmed his realization that trying to protect his heart was ridiculous. It was already too late.

The lawmen, having spent the night interviewing Ridge and Agnew, gave the bounty hunters answers to their most pressing questions.

"Kris Ridge came to Blue Mountain to hide immediately after he jumped bail fifteen years ago," Silva said. "He checked around and eventually discovered that Virgil Agnew's wife was very ill and could easily guess that the family needed money. Ridge approached him at a vulnerable moment and offered him the money he needed for his wife in return for protection from the cops. Before Virgil knew it, he was locked into a situation that he couldn't see his way out of."

Katherine shook her head sadly.

"What was his connection with Barry Foster, exactly?" Hayley asked. "He mentioned something about drug dealing last night."

"Right. So Ridge didn't just hide out here in Blue Mountain," Silva answered. "He used some of his money to start a drug distribution network. We knew drugs were becoming a bigger issue in town, but we had no clue that was connected to Kris Ridge.

"Barry Foster's two thug friends had experience in that illegal kind of work, and Foster thought he'd escape to Blue Mountain and set up his business here. I'm not sure if he even knew that he'd be stepping on Ridge's toes when he did that. But Ridge cared. He knew Foster was a wanted man, and Ridge was determined to do something to anonymously get Foster captured. He started tailing Foster and he saw his chance to take him out of competition. You were there when it happened."

"So he was deliberately trying to help us capture Foster?" Hayley asked.

Silva nodded.

"You know, I had my suspicions about you." Jack turned to Parker, who hadn't said much so far. "Right up until the very end."

The patrolman smiled. "Yeah, I know. I had my suspicions about you, too. A few months after I got hired, I heard rumors about Agnew and wondered if they were true. I talked to former Blue Mountain cops who told me about their uneasiness, about their efforts to fight crime being occasionally undermined and how there'd been steady departmental personnel turnover for several years.

"Chief Silva and I had begun trying to get a handle on what was going on. We wondered if there were dirty cops on the payroll. And when you bounty hunters showed up, I started out on the assumption that you were unethical and part of the crime problem. And I was happy to find out that I was wrong."

"Glad I was wrong about you, too," Jack said.

After an exchange of pleasantries, the lawmen left.

A short time later, Katherine and Milo grabbed their bags, set them by the door and then hugged Hayley goodbye. They told her how much they'd enjoyed working with her, and then they were gone, too. Without offering Jack a ride home, he noted.

So that left Jack with Hayley.

Hayley was already packed. It didn't take Jack long to take care of that task and then he was ready to go, too.

Except part of him really *wasn't* so ready. He set his bag down outside his bedroom door, and then turned his gaze around the shared area of the suite where he and Hayley had lived and worked so closely together. It had only been for a handful of days, but so much had happened during that time.

Not all of it related to the chase for fugitives.

Much as he didn't think of himself as a sentimental guy, it was hard to just walk out of the suite. And then, after arriving home in Range River, going their separate ways.

But he didn't know what else he could do. If he told Hayley how he felt, if he brought up their kiss in the forest, would that bring them together or push her away. Would it be too much too soon? Because he *thought* it was. And yet he *knew* it was true. He knew beyond a shadow of a doubt how he felt.

She started to move toward him as he reached down to pick up his duffel bag, moving awkwardly because of his injured leg. "I'm getting around like an old man," he joked self-consciously.

"I don't care that you're older than me," Hayley said, the earnestness in her eyes giving him a surge of hope that he could barely contain.

He dropped the bag and moved toward her. "I definitely don't think you're a kid."

He reached out to trace his finger along the side of her face and under her chin. She blushed, and he actually felt like he might be blushing, too.

She took a deep breath. "Okay, this is always a risky thing for anyone to say." She gave him a shy and teasing smile. "But since I'm a person who can handle living on the edge, I'll say it first."

"I love you," Jack said at the exact same time that she spoke the words.

Hayley burst out laughing. And then, slowly, her gaze grew serious.

He felt his own gaze turn serious as he reached out, pulled her close to him and pressed his lips to hers. The old fear of giving his heart to another person melted completely away. The feeling of joy that took its place nearly overwhelmed him as Haley pulled him even closer, her warm touch giving him a sense of completeness that he couldn't remember ever feeling before.

# EPILOGUE

*Seven months later*

"It isn't very far from here to the Riverside Inn," Hayley said to her oldest brother, Connor, as he focused his dark-eyed gaze on her and frowned. "And I'm still going to be working for Range River Bail Bonds," she continued. "You'll still see me nearly every day."

They were standing on Jack Colter's property—well, legally, now Hayley's property, too. Their wedding had been held at the Still Waters Church in downtown Range River a couple of hours ago. Now the reception was being held on Jack's—and Hayley's—horse ranch in the rolling hills on the southern outskirts of town.

Hayley's brothers, Connor, Danny and Wade—she considered Wade a brother even though they weren't blood relatives—had promised to behave themselves and not harass their new brother-in-law *too* much. They'd kept their word, and directed their teasing at Hayley instead. Mostly reminding her that she'd better not forget her family now that she was a married woman living on this beautiful property.

Of course she wasn't going to forget her family. Their worries that she was somehow going to be taken away from them were ridiculous. She'd wanted the reception to be here at the ranch to make that exact point. She wasn't taking anything away from the tight bond her family shared, but rather adding to it. They would be welcome here at the ranch anytime. Her new husband, who'd turned out to have more patience with her rowdy relatives than she could have imagined, was the first one to tell them that.

Maribel Fast Horse, who stood beside Connor, caught Hayley's gaze and then rolled her eyes and laughed. Hayley's sister-in-law, Tanya, married to Hayley's brother Danny, likewise appeared amused. It didn't seem like very long ago when Hayley had needed to let Tanya know that while the Ryan–Fast Horse clan could sometimes seem overbearing, it was because their love and concern made them that way.

Luther Garcia walked by behind Connor, saw Hayley and smiled and waved. He'd recovered nicely from that horrible ambush in the forest in Blue Mountain.

Jack excused himself from talking to one of his friends, stepped closer to Hayley, took her hand and kissed it. "Pardon us," he said smoothly to Connor as he drew his new bride away to dance as the band started a slow-moving country song.

The more time Jack and Hayley spent together, the more she felt like he had mellowed. Not as a bounty hunter—in that regard he was as fierce as ever—but living his life, in not seeming so compelled to constantly prove himself.

Hayley knew that she'd grown and changed, as well. She was less defensive and, like Jack, didn't feel so driven to "win" every argument or challenge. Learning to trust someone could do that to a person. To a couple. Even if at the beginning they had only been pretending to be a couple.

The ranch's biggest barn had been cleared out and decorated for the reception. Jack and Hayley moved easily over the wooden floor as they danced together. In tune with one another. Their futures interwound.

"I think we're going to have to give your brothers bedrooms in the house here so they can keep an eye on you and won't worry," Jack said teasingly.

Hayley laughed. "Nah. They're tough. We can just get them tents."

Jack chuckled, pulled her closer and spun her around. She glanced over his shoulder at their friends and family. A sense of competition between Jack and her brothers would probably always be there, to some degree, because of the type of men they were. But that strength of character, balanced with love, would serve them all well and make them stronger.

Hayley let herself relax in Jack's arms, grateful for the love and grace that had brought the two of them, and their families, together.

\* \* \* \* \*

Dear Reader,

I love romances that start with the hero and heroine not particularly liking one another. I remember seeing an older movie version of *Pride and Prejudice* when I was young and loving it. It's so fun to watch two characters with undeniable chemistry between them slowly become aware of their mistaken assumptions and begin to see the other person for who they truly are.

It was fun playing with that idea as I followed Hayley and Jack on the hunt for their fugitives. Of course they found their bad guys, but beyond that, they *found* each other. A nice bonus!

Next up from the Range River Bounty Hunters crew will be Wade Fast Horse. This honorary brother in the Ryan family is willing to hunt bad guys and fight to keep a woman safe, but it's purely business. He's cynical and immune to romance. Or so he thinks.

I invite you to visit my website, Jenna-Night.com, where you can keep up with my book releases and sign up for my newsletter. I also have a Jenna Night Facebook Page and you can follow me on BookBub. My email address is Jenna@JennaNight.com. I'd love to hear from you.

Regards,
*Jenna*

# COUNTRY LEGACY COLLECTION

**19 FREE BOOKS IN ALL!**

Cowboys, adventure and romance await you in this new collection! Enjoy superb reading all year long with books by bestselling authors like Diana Palmer, Sasha Summers and Marie Ferrarella!